# The Fall

Laura Liddell Nolen grew up in Hattiesburg, Mississippi. She has a degree in French and a license to practice law, but both are frozen in carbonite at present. She lives in Texas with her husband and two young children. Laura can be found on Twitter @LauraLLNolen.

Also by Laura Liddell Nolen

**The Ark Trilogy**
*The Ark*
*The Remnant*

# The Fall

# LAURA LIDDELL NOLEN

## Book Three of The Ark Trilogy

HARPER
Voyager

HarperVoyager
An imprint of HarperCollinsPublishers Ltd
1 London Bridge Street
London SE1 9GF

www.harpercollins.co.uk

This paperback edition 2018

First published in Great Britain in ebook format by
HarperCollinsPublishers 2018

A catalogue record for this book
is available from the British Library

ISBN: 978-0-00-818148-2

Set in Sabon by
Palimpsest Book Production Limited, Falkirk, Stirlingshire

Printed and bound by CPI Group (UK) Ltd, Croydon, CR0 4YY

*For Oscar*

Others, so far as I can understand, have been taken by him, as well as we; and yet have escaped out of his hand. Who knows, but the God that made the world may cause that Giant Despair may die? or that, at some time or other, he may forget to lock us in?

—*The Pilgrim's Progress*

# One

The first time I tried to kill Adam, I tasted sugar.

We weren't alone. We never were. A tightly-wound shadow flinched behind my left shoulder every time I moved my arm, threatening to make itself fully known, but I couldn't give it a name, so I ignored it, even though it made my ribs shake and my fingers cold.

Adam rolled a chair from behind the desk, remaining seated, and I could only stare. Clean brown hair, like he'd combed it twice. Dark eyes on pale skin, like his sister. I blinked. Something was different.

"Chew, Char. Maybe next year, I'll let you blow the candles out."

I looked down. A mountain of pink icing covered the plate in my lap. A cake stood between us, tall and bright, and missing two slices. The world was obscured behind a thick pane of hazy glass, with only Adam in focus.

So I stared at him instead, trying to figure out where I was, and why.

We were in a control room, I decided, judging by all the shiny panels, and it was someone's birthday. My good arm, as I thought of it, held a fork. My wrist on my good arm had light bruises, like I'd been yanking it against a handcuff.

My bad arm had no bruises. But then, it had no wrist, either, since it ended below the elbow. At least they couldn't cuff it. I frowned. That wasn't much of a silver lining.

I was pretty sure I'd been here before. I knew, for instance, that this wasn't the first birthday I'd celebrated with Adam, that the door was behind me, and that I didn't care about anything on the console to my immediate right.

Or maybe I'd just figured that out a moment ago. I couldn't tell.

The twitchy shadow-person stepped around to see why I wasn't chewing despite having a mouth full of cake, and we squinted at each other as she came briefly into view. She looked to be around thirty, with amber skin and short black hair untouched by streaks of gray. There was a sour tension around her mouth. She didn't like me.

No, no. That wasn't it. I wrenched myself around to inspect her again. She stepped away from my line of sight without catching my eye.

She didn't like Adam, I decided. Me, she didn't think about at all.

"She's fine. A little tired, maybe," she said.

"Let's wake her up some more," said Adam.

"Too dangerous, unless you want to cuff her. Remember last time?"

"No cuff. I want her to eat the cake." He looked disappointed, but returned his attention to me. "Give me that napkin."

*I will not. I want to throw him out an airlock.* Why would I—

I extended the napkin toward him, and he snatched it with an appraising glance. "Not feeling too feisty today, huh? I can live with that," he said. "Long as you behave. Have some more."

I had an overwhelming urge to stab him. It was related to the story he was telling, but I knew I wasn't supposed to think about that.

What was I supposed to do? I bit a lip, confounded, and tasted blood. It wasn't enough to wake me up, so I pressed the tines of the fork into my thigh. The urge to stab grew stronger. I needed to wake up a little more. I *had* to. I wasn't sure why, though.

Maybe it would help if I went ahead and stabbed him?

No, no. That wasn't it. I shook my head, but it didn't clear.

Maybe I was supposed to eat the cake, and *then* stab him? Or maybe I should give him another napkin. It was kind of a toss-up, honestly.

"Hey, don't look so down. It's your birthday, after all. Why d'you think we got pink icing? The Lieutenant prefers chocolate." He laughed, as if it were a joke.

*I'm not eating his stupid cake. I don't even want cake. I hate strawberry.*

To my surprise, I lifted my fork. It was indeed covered in bright pink icing, and I shook my head a little harder. Birthday cakes should be blue. Like West's.

I worked my mouth around the load of frosting. It was sweet—too sweet—and I forced myself to swallow. Fine: cake first, then stab. Surely that was a solid plan.

Wasn't it?

"That's better," Adam was saying. "Now. Where were we? Yeah, your family. 'Fraid it's bad news, Char. Let me see if I can remember exactly where we left off last year." He shifted comfortably, and I got another look at his face.

"Oh, right. It was the part where you let my sister die."

I blinked. He was different. Not how I remembered him. The soft, round parts of his boyish face were now angular. Angry. "I didn't kill—"

"Hey, hey. Cut it out. Every year, it's the same thing. *But Aah—dam!*" he whined, imitating my voice. "*I didn't kill her! Blah, blah, lightning clouds. Blah, blah, mutiny.* We haven't even gotten to the good part yet!" His eyes flashed, and he waved at the woman. "Wake her up a little more. I need her to remember this one." They exchanged a glance. "Do it, Lieutenant."

"Yes, sir," she said, a touch of strain in her voice. A sting spread through my right bicep, and I felt my heart speed up. I started breathing faster.

My mind began to clear.

I was in Central Command, and Adam was the Commander. He was in league with An Zhao, who had recently blown a hole in the Ark, destroying the Remnant, the group of free thinkers who'd built a city and organized a government in the bowels of the ship. And I had disarmed us to prevent her from doing worse. I had made us helpless. My fingers tightened around the fork. I had to get out of here.

Every year, we ate cake.

Every year, he woke me up to hear the story.

Every year, I had ten minutes to work on my plan. Tick, tock.

If only I could remember what it was.

I couldn't remember much of anything, to be honest. "Are—are we there yet?" I asked.

"Where? Eirenea?" Adam laughed, but there was steel in the sound. "No. Don't interrupt."

He had the relaxed posture of a person in control, but he wore it uneasily, as though he were copying something he'd seen another man do. My head rolled around slightly while I tried to think. There was nothing easy in his face. His teeth were clenched so hard that he had to move his jaw around before speaking. "And so my sister died in your arms," he was saying. "And I'm not sure whether we covered this last year, but she was all I had. And she needed me." He leaned forward. "And you let her die."

If I had made us helpless, Adam had returned the favor tenfold. I spent my days in a cloud of confusion, blindly following any instructions I was given. I wasn't dizzy, exactly, but I had a hard time getting my bearings. Every so often, I came to my senses, and Adam would be there. Sometimes he just wanted to talk. Sometimes he didn't speak at all.

But sometimes, he taunted me. On these occasions, there was cake. Always pink.

And I had to eat it. And he told me a story I shouldn't hear while I plotted ways to kill him. Usually with a fork.

Not everyone on the Ark was drugged. Eren, as far as I knew, spent most of his days in InterArk Comm Con, sending and receiving transmissions related to the Ark's operations. The last time I tried to contact him had not gone well. I stumbled into the amphitheater, stupid from the drugs. I saw Eren, his eyes wide, his head shaking back and forth, subtly at first, and then more urgently.

And then I awoke in the commissary six months later, half a sandwich hanging from my mouth, without even the slightest memory of any medication top-ups that must have taken place since.

I didn't try that again.

So I was on my own. Adam sat back, warming to his

story. "But all was not lost! Not quite yet. Not for you, Char. They say all's fair in love and war, but that's never been my experience. The Academy, for example, was not fair. They took me when I was five. Did you hear that? Five, Char. And my parents just *let* them."

The Academy was a school for certain children from all over the world selected to survive the meteor. They were trained in science, medicine, or engineering at an early age, so that they would be as useful as possible on board the Arks.

Unbeknownst to the people set to die in their place, they were also trained in military strategy. And combat.

"Sounds rough," I said. My voice cracked from disuse. I had a hard time feeling sorry for anyone chosen for a place on an Ark when all the rest of us were left to die in the meteor strike.

"They took her, too. Same age. What do you think they did to her at the Academy? They didn't want students. I'll tell you that. Because everything there was a weapon. Especially us. Tell me something, Char. What were all those weapons *for* if no one was supposed to use them?"

His voice trailed off, and he gave me a long look before continuing. "And I escaped. Obviously. And I found her. And I made sure she lived, Char. Because that was my job. To protect her." He glanced around the room. "Eat."

I ate.

"You should know something about that, Char. Being abandoned? Protecting your family? And you did a great job; you really did. They escaped!" He smiled darkly. "For a few minutes, anyway."

This was the part I wasn't supposed to listen to. Every year, same thing. Adam woke me up and told the same

6

story. And I made the same mistake every time I heard it. First, the blood would rush through my ears, drowning my plan in panic. And then my chest would squeeze. And then I started screaming.

And then he'd smile and knock me out again.

But this year would be different. This year, I had a job to do.

If only I could remember what it was.

I needed one more shot of whatever the Lieutenant had given me. Then maybe I would remember.

I lowered my head and spoke in a soft monotone. "You knew about my father's Arkhopper, and you blew it up. They're all dead. My family is dead."

Adam took a long pause, then slowly reached for the holster where he kept the drug. I braced myself for oblivion. Another year lost.

But instead, he straightened his jacket and shook his head, annoyed. "No. That's not her. That's not what I want. Wake her up some more. I want the real Char."

The woman straightened. "But sir—"

"Now, Lieutenant. Do it now, or we can continue this conversation next year. When I wake *you* up."

There was a rustling of equipment behind me as the Lieutenant rushed to comply. Another sting in my arm. Another breath, and it all came crashing back.

I was definitely supposed to stab him.

# Two

"So there I was, minding my own business in my new office on the Guardian Level, when I got news that the Commander was dead. Thanks for that, by the way," Adam nodded at me. "I wasn't sure I had the nerve until that moment. They need me, you know. This Ark." He leaned in. "They know it, and I know it. They need someone who can keep a sense of order around here."

The Commander had had control of the Guardians, and he'd wielded them like his own personal army in a failed attempt to retain control over the Ark and to crush the Remnant, a hidden group of survivors who opposed him.

Oh, and he was also Eren's father.

Eren. Blue eyes. Security, like a thick blue blanket. A fleeting moment of happiness from a silver ring with a pale blue stone. But there was something dark in my memories of Eren, too. My thoughts pressed themselves forward all at once and without a coherent order. I rubbed my leg nervously, trying to clear my mind, but they kept coming. Green pins of light and a red expanse of blood. His father had died by my hand. Surely I hadn't meant for that to happen, had I? I wondered where Eren was. Hadn't I sent him away?

I wondered if he missed his father in spite of everything he'd put us through.

Wait, *stop*. Stabbing. I needed to focus on stabbing now.

"Hope Eren didn't take it too hard. So I thought to myself, Adam, we're doing all right. Everything's coming together. Isaiah may not ever come around, but we're better off without him anyway. The only way the Remnant was going to achieve equal footing was by blowing everything up and starting over."

He crossed his legs, studying my face. The fork was light in my hand. I shifted my grip without looking down.

"But you, Char. You were different. I thought, I can explain myself to her, and she'll listen. Maybe not at first. But she understands what it's like, being ignored. Being feared. She'll know what to do. I didn't even *want* to kill Isaiah, Char. Honest. The Remnant—the whole thing was his idea in the first place. It wouldn't have been right.

"You didn't have to be my enemy. But then Amiel was dead. And you walked right into my trap." His head tilted. "And I decided to change tack."

"You're lying," I said. "My family isn't dead. The Remnant isn't—"

"There she is!" Adam sat up straight. "Welcome back, Char. It's been a long, hard year without you."

"If you're trying to scare me, give it up, Adam. I'm not afraid anymore."

"A return to form!" Adam clapped. "This really is exciting. Can I tell you their last words?"

*Don't listen. Don't listen. Don't*—I breathed in measured beats. Steady. I had a job to do.

"Do you ever wonder whether they were talking about you? Worried for you? I don't think we got this far last year."

*Don't listen dontlistendontlisten.* I breathed a little faster. The handle of the fork bit into my palm.

Adam leaned in, exposing the softest part of his neck, and lowered his voice to deliver another blow. "They didn't die right away, you know. There was screaming."

I rushed him, arm high, and made a sound like a burning pterodactyl. He jumped, predictably, and I drove the fork into his neck.

Or at least, I tried to.

At the last instant, a blunt weight tackled me from the left. I hit the floor harder than I expected. For some reason, I was unable to break my fall.

That's when I remembered that my right arm ended just below the elbow, and I howled again, angry. Helpless.

The sound of Adam's laughter filled my mind, and the Lieutenant shuffled me onto my back. She was armed in an instant.

I saw the needle coming for me, but Adam stayed his hand, savoring a final moment with me, his favorite prisoner.

"We can make this stop, you know. Tell me what happened to Ark Five, and I might let you stay awake this year."

"Why does everyone keep *asking* me that? Seriously, I have no idea."

The control room was like a slippery plastic slide, and I had the intense feeling of falling into a void beneath it. "Happy birthday, Char. And many happy returns."

The corners of my brain went dark and began to expand. With my last cogent thought, I focused on the weight of the Lieutenant on my chest as she scrambled to secure my bad arm, which was pressing into her throat. Her breathing leveled off as I came under her control, but so did mine.

She'd landed right where I wanted her. I focused my last seconds of consciousness into my remaining hand, which was already halfway to the black pack she carried across her flank, just under the flap of her uniform jacket, until my fingers touched steel. I hoped that she was a moment too late, that her nerves had made her overly concerned about the fork. I hoped desperately that I hadn't dreamed the last few moments. That I wasn't dreaming already.

And then, my moment was spent.

The slide grew steeper, and the Lieutenant relaxed her grip on my upper body. There was nothing left but the fall. My latest prison had no cells, no bars, and no hope of escape. So I couldn't say I'd ever enjoyed the trip into mental stasis.

But this time, I smiled the whole way down.

# Three

In my dream, my mother held my hands—both of them—but she looked like Meghan Notting, the gritty old woman who'd died helping me escape Earth. I shook my head, trying to fix her face back, and in response, she offered me a screen stem.

It was almost black, like graphite, but harder, and bluntly tapered on one end. I recognized it immediately because it was covered in blood: Jorin's. I pictured his ugly, sneering face and backed away. I didn't regret killing him. I didn't. But that didn't stop me from thinking on the moment in horror whenever I fell asleep.

My mother-Meghan moved toward my face, and I resisted the urge to run. I could not account for her appearance as Meghan, but I knew that she was my mother all the same. Did this version of her have an open wound where Cassa had shot her? I looked away. I didn't want to know.

Perhaps it didn't matter. Perhaps the dead felt no pain.

"Your leg, sweetheart," she said softly, pressing the stem into my palm. I picked it up with my other hand, the one from my bad arm.

"Mom, no."

"Use this hand." She put it back in my other hand, the one on my good arm, and closed my fingers around the sticky weapon.

"That's gonna hurt. I stabbed someone with a stem before, Mom. It hurts."

"Only the dead feel no pain, Charlotte. Your life was never meant to be so precious."

A flare of anger. "You're just saying what I've been thinking. You're not even real."

She started at a noise, then looked behind her. Her hair in my face was suddenly like my mother's, long and dark, and I needed her to hold me. "Now, Charlotte," she said. "Do it now."

"Mom. I'm afraid."

And then she did embrace me, and I was warm, and her hair smelled like I remembered.

But she was only a dream.

In real life, I had no mother. I had no right hand, either.

I lifted the screen stem in my left hand. She nodded approvingly.

I drove it deep into my leg, and when the pain came, I sucked it in through every pore. When I screamed, I breathed out the scent of her hair forever. It was my mother's voice that shrieked, but I held fast to the red sensation taking root in my thigh, and my dream-mother grew distant.

This pain was mine alone.

"Charlotte. Hey. Wake up." Eren's face hovered over mine, awash in concern. "You're having a nightmare."

I rubbed my face and tried to get my bearings. I was sitting precariously on the edge of a bed, half-wrapped in a warm comforter. Navy blue. "Not exactly."

"You okay?"

"How did you get in here? How did you find me?"

He was unsurprised by the question and spoke slowly, as if I were a child. "I live here. We live together, remember? Officially, anyway. You're in our bed."

I raised an eyebrow. "Our—what now?"

He reevaluated my coherency and adopted a less irritating tone. "I've been sleeping next door. The rooms are connected through the kitchen." He waved an arm.

I stood up, intending to investigate, but he stopped me immediately.

"Woah." His eyes here huge, and I followed his gaze to my thigh.

An empty syringe dangled from my bare leg.

I took a breath and pulled it out.

His eyes bulged nearly out of his head, but he put a finger to his lips, shushing me. I nodded wearily and began to limp around the room. It was cold, so I dragged the comforter with me. I lacked the energy to wrap it around me, so I just hugged it to my chest. It felt good.

The kitchen was just as I remembered it, but I did not recall the door, or the little room behind it.

It was pale yellow, with a generic-looking painting of a lamb grazing in a green pasture. There was a fluffy white rug in the center, just next to a tiny bed surrounded by bars. I frowned. The bars on the bed were decorated with ribbons.

Wait, that wasn't a bed. Not exactly.

I turned back to Eren, who'd followed me. "You sleep in a *crib*?"

"I kinda put the mattress on the floor, and my legs hang over the—you know what? That's not important right now."

"Why?"

"Because you get a little stabby when you're sleeping."

"That." I pointed. "That is a *nursery*." My hand went to my belly, and I searched my memory for evidence of a pregnancy. Not that I knew what that might involve, but nothing came to mind.

"You never—we never—Char, nothing happened. They made it a nursery for appearances. This was a long time ago."

"You're not that naïve. It's just a matter of time, Eren. Adam gets bored. He'll want a new toy."

"He insisted," Eren said. "He controls everything."

"Yeah. Kinda worked that one out already." I leaned in and lowered my voice. "Eren, this room is bugged. It's gotta be."

He shrugged and spoke normally. "It is. I found four."

"That means there are at least eight, and two of them probably aren't even electronic."

"That's what you said last time," he said mildly.

"*Last time?* Catch me up a little faster, here."

He shrugged, and I had the impression that he was trying to force his voice to sound bored. "You wake up like this every so often. We talk, and you go back into stasis. I don't think it bothers him."

I slid the door to the nursery firmly shut and leaned against the formica counter in the kitchen. A cold prickle waved through the back of my skull. "Eren, how long have I been... asleep?"

He rubbed the side of his head, looking pained. "Well, technically, it's not sleep; it's more like stasis. The body ages, but the mind—"

"How long, Eren."

"You always ask this. It's not going to—"

"How. Long."

He met my eye. "Five years."

Reeling, I put out a hand. He grabbed it, steadying me, but released me as soon as I had my balance.

Five years.

Five years of droning on through meaningless, mindless tasks in Central Command, unable to form memories or connections, while the Arks barreled on toward Eirenea. Five years of listening to Adam talk, of hearing his taunts. Of watching him build a great and merciless empire on board the Ark.

Five years of a lifeless "marriage" to Eren, who clearly no longer returned my affections.

Five years of planning my escape.

It seemed to me that it had passed overnight, but I read the exhaustion in Eren's face, and I knew that what we'd once had together was long adrift, gone to sea. No one loves a puppet.

That had been my choice, too. Before all of this, I'd told Eren that we couldn't be together anymore, that we had bigger things to focus on. That I had to become more than a daughter, or even a wife. So I set him free.

And judging by the speed with which his hand had pulled away from mine, he was free indeed.

"That makes me... twenty-two years old."

I heard a note of panic rising up in my voice, but Eren just stared at me like he'd seen this scene play out before.

"Eren, I have to get out of here."

"You say that, too," he said quietly.

"I have to find my family. Do I say that?"

He gave me a sympathetic nod. "Then you won't let me

16

stay with you. You get back in bed. But you keep the light on all night, like you're trying to stay awake."

I hobbled over to his wardrobe, leaving the blanket on the cold floor. Maybe he had a pair of pants I could wear if I rolled the legs up.

The row of uniforms perfectly tailored to my size was like a slap in the face. I yanked one down and stepped into it angrily, pulling it up over my hips and around my nightshirt. Of course they fit me. They were my clothes. I lived here. Eren moved to help with the zipper, but I shrugged him off angrily. It took longer, but I'd far rather put on my own clothes than accept one more second of his sympathy.

I yanked my ID card off the mattress and pulled Eren's shoulder down towards mine, so that I could whisper directly into his ear. Maybe Adam had planted a bug right inside Eren's head, and I'd never be free of him. Maybe his Lieutenant noticed the syringe I'd swiped, and he was waiting for me just outside the door. At that moment, I didn't even care. I was furious. "I'm leaving," I muttered. "Right now. And you can come or not; I don't care." I pulled away, meeting his gaze with fire. "Have I ever said *that* before?"

I let my eyes glass over as we marched through the hall. The next phase of my plan was significantly less clear. "So," I muttered, "my plan is to sneak into InterArk Comm Con and ping Europe."

"Not gonna work," he whispered back. "They know what's going on. They don't care."

More like, they'd rather leave it alone so we can all get to Eirenea in one piece. Not that I blamed them. From their perspective, Adam had presided over five years of relative peace. Left alone, he was no threat to any ship but his own. "So we'll make them care."

"Charlotte."

The warning in his tone was clear, and I could guess what he was thinking. If I failed, he had another year of waiting to look forward to. Another year under Adam's thumb. His age had increased tenfold in the dark circles beneath his eyes. Eren had felt every minute of the years I'd lost in the space of a single dream.

"Have a little faith," I said lightly, speeding up to brush past an oncoming group. "I don't intend to get caught," I muttered. "But I can't just let a twelve-year-old despot control my brain forever."

"He's seventeen, now," Eren said softly.

"They grow up so fast."

We marched the rest of the way in silence, greeted by the occasional nod to Eren. I was ignored. "How many people has he drugged like this?"

"Unclear," he murmured. "But you're the only one who's consistently under. He's used it on others. Any one he sees as a threat, of course, and anyone he wants to punish."

"You?"

His focus slid back to the hallway. "No."

I barely had time to wonder why Adam never saw Eren as a threat when the door sucked open. Comm Con was much as I remembered it, floating stars and all. This was the place where I'd married Eren. It was where we'd shared our first kiss, and our last.

I half-lowered my eyelids in an attempt to look like I was still in stasis, but no one paid any attention to me. The enormous black amphitheater had maybe four other people, and no one was near the control desk.

"New plan. We ping my dad."

I couldn't miss the look of alarm that hit his face, or the care he took to hide it.

"He's not dead, if that's what you're worried about," I whispered.

"Don't let them see you talking. Nothing coherent, anyway."

I angled my face away from the others. "He's not dead. Adam wouldn't have made such a big deal out of it all the time if that were the case."

Eren avoided my gaze with the precision of a fighter pilot. "Adam had no reason not to kill him, Charlotte. And there was opportunity, motive."

"I'm not sure about that. It was chaos the day of the attack." I should know. As far as I was concerned, it happened yesterday. "He had a strike team after him, and his Remnant headquarters were obliterated, obviously. There was a big lag between when he lost Isaiah and when you and I got here, which was when he had control of the speaker system." I paused, reliving the moment, and sucked in a deep breath. "And the oxygen."

Eren settled himself at his desk, and I sat, robot-like, in a nearby chair.

"Anyway," I continued, monotone, "I'm not totally convinced he'd take the shot even if he had it. He didn't know Amiel was dead at that point."

"Depends on when your dad tried to leave, doesn't it?" said Eren. "And let's just agree to disagree on whether he'd take the shot either way. But here's the real problem: you *can't* ping him. You don't know where he is."

He had me there. I had no way of knowing where they'd gone.

But I had a pretty good guess.

"Is there a shipment or anything headed toward the European Ark today? I assume we have a good relationship with them, right?"

"To the extent that you could call it a relationship, yes. Adam sends them things from time to time. Usually tech-related. They reciprocate. A bunch of our doctors disappeared right after he started drugging people. There was talk of a strike among the medics, but instead, they just vanished. When our sick bay filled up, Europe stepped in."

"Europe sent us *doctors*? Willingly?"

"No, they refuse to give him any personnel. But they accept patients."

I glanced around the room. By some miracle, no one was paying any attention to us. I guess after five years of puppet-hood, I had become completely invisible. Predictable, even.

I could work with that.

"So," I said softly. "When's the next shipment of patients going out?"

"Not for another week."

A week. That was a long time to dodge Adam. "I don't think I can wait that long. He'll know something's up any minute now. Certainly by morning."

"I don't see that you have any choice. You can't stay here," he said, his voice more urgent than before. "He's going to drug you again."

"Look who's suddenly on Team Char."

"The way I see it, you need to get off this Ark. You can't hide here. No one can. We have to depose Adam before we land. If he drugs you again, that's another year gone. We'll miss our window. Get out. Get some support. Come back and stage a coup."

20

Five years ago, Eren would never have dreamed of supporting a coup. I had the sudden, slippery feeling that I was talking to a stranger, that I'd lost something I cared for, and I shivered. I couldn't think about that right now. "I can't possibly—"

"If anyone can do it, it's you."

"Is there even any support still left around here? Maybe people *want* Adam in charge. I mean, he destroyed the Remnant and overthrew the Commander. He's probably not anyone's first choice, but you never know."

"I have no idea," said Eren. "No one talks to me. I'm too close to Adam. And I'm married to you, remember? You're not exactly popular with either group, either, you know."

He was probably referring to the fact that I'd killed the Commander and betrayed Isaiah, putting me squarely at odds with both Central Command and the Remnant. That would also account for the depressing fact that in five years, no one had bothered rescuing me, rebellion or not.

"Can you arrange another patient transport? Say, tonight?"

"Charlotte. We have no allies. No resources."

"Aren't you the Lieutenant Commander? I seem to remember something about that from my hospital stay."

He gave me a long look, then turned back to fiddle with the control panel. "I was, for a little while. The position changed hands a few years ago."

"Yeah, yeah. I met her. Early thirties, kinda stabby, likes to play with needles? Arms like a bear trap."

"No. I mean, yes, she's the real LC. But that's a secret. Officially, on paper, it's someone else."

"Anyone I know?" I scanned my brain for candidates,

but Eren had stopped dinking around and sat still instead, staring at the constellation hologram. It was disconcerting. "Earth to Eren."

"Yeah, Char. It's you."

I snorted. "Me."

"Lieutenant Everest," he said, using our married name. His voice was blank, but there was a sad softness in his eyes that made me reach for his hand. He pulled away, and I whisked air. It was like falling through an unseen crack in the middle of a familiar street.

"Eren, please. We can't just—"

"Lieutenant!" a voice pierced our conversation, and I forced myself not to jump.

"Mnmm." I glanced up sleepily. A uniformed man strode toward us, insignia blazing, and my hand wandered toward the emblems on my own uniform. His mouth concealed a sneer. It hit me that he'd probably been in the military all his life, and I, to all the world an idiot, outranked him. Adam played a dangerous game.

He saluted, an action I did not return, and a look of disdain, or pity, crept over his face. "Inform the High Commander that the day's operations are completed."

Now, how in the heck was I supposed to talk to Adam?

I sat there, dumb as a stump, until Eren laid a hand on mine. It was warm, and for a moment, I felt secure again. "Here," he said, his voice gentle and slow. He slid my fingers across the control panel in front of us and pressed my finger over an iridescent plate an inch wide. Fingerprint scanner, I supposed. "InterArk Comm Con to headquarters."

There was a pause, then a rustle, and Adam spoke.

"Command."

The two men looked at me, and I used my best sleepy

22

voice. "The day's operations are complete. Comp-leted," I corrected myself with a slur.

"Dismiss the crew. Send her over, Everest," came the reply. "Command out."

The man in uniform scoffed and trooped away.

The crew filed out of the room without a second glance at me, and when the door closed behind them, Eren cleared his throat. "So."

"So," I replied expectantly. "Ideas. Thinking. We need a plan." He continued to look at me, and I felt a little trill of panic. "Quickly, please."

"You're wanted at headquarters," he said.

I stared at him. "Yeah. That's why the hurry, slick." A look I couldn't place crossed over his face, and I felt myself get angry. He still wouldn't meet my eye. Another moment passed, and my hands went cold. I was finally free from stasis. *Why was he just sitting there?* "Look, Eren. I know I can't imagine what you've been through in the last five years, but please. Get it together. If Adam figures out that I'm awake right now, he'll put me under for another year. That can't be what you really want." I heard my voice crack, and it sounded like it belonged to someone else. "Surely."

"Charlotte," he said gently. "He's—"

"Don't *Charlotte* me. I am not going back to him. I have to... I have to get out of here."

Another moment went by. Was he afraid the room was bugged? I leaned in to whisper, for whatever that was worth. "Eren. I'm leaving. With or without you. And the next time I go back to Adam, it'll be to stop him. For good."

He looked at me, slack-jawed, but said nothing. *What was wrong with him?*

My breath came shorter. I'd have to do this without him.

Well, maybe it didn't matter. I had survived on the run before. Granted, Adam was smarter and more prepared than anyone else I'd ever run from, but I couldn't let that scare me. I would rather die than spend another minute under his spell.

I stood angrily, knocking my chair backwards, and stalked out of the room.

My face burned beneath my skin. So much for Eren Everest. Adam was a threat to everything I'd ever cared about. If Eren thought I would go back to him, or if he thought for one second that I would somehow play nice until we got to Eirenea, then he never knew me at all.

# Four

My first order of business was to get good and hidden. I jogged about halfway down the hall before the sound of footsteps jarred me back to reality, and I forced my pace to slow. If I were going to make it through this, I needed to look like a puppet.

A pair of officers walked past, giving me ample space on the carpet lining the center of the floor. I let my gaze drift idly to the chandeliers overhead. They'd sustained a fair amount of damage during the loss of gravity following An's torpedo, but someone had taken the time to rehang them, untangling their delicate strings of crystals. They were repaired as well as could be expected. I shifted my focus away. It wasn't like you could replace something like that up here. There were no craftworkers in Central Command, anyway. The officers passed, and I paused, listening for more footsteps, then took off running again.

It wasn't until I got all the way to the door that I realized that I had nowhere to go. Subconsciously, I'd been heading for the stairwell and the cargo space beneath the main part of the ship. But it no longer existed, and whatever was left of it wasn't pressurized. The next thought that hit me was worse: the Remnant was gone, too.

*I owe you for that one, An. I haven't forgotten.*

I endured a crippling moment of panic before I finally understood that I had no real options. My only hope was to delay my return to Adam as long as could be believable, and hope I came up with some kind of a plan before he caught on. Which wouldn't be long.

A weapon would be a good start. Something I could hide in my sleeve.

Eren seemed pretty tight with Adam. Did Adam trust him enough to let him carry a gun? I hadn't seen one on him, so I decided to search his room. If I got caught, I could always act like I'd wandered in out of habit. After all, it was my room, too, apparently.

The room smelled good in spite of the sterility of space and the crumpled pile of clothes near the door. Peppermint and toasted bread. I shrugged it off and got to work.

A cursory search revealed no gun in his desk, or under the bed, or anywhere in the wardrobe. I grunted and sat back on my heels to think. I was a thief, after all. This shouldn't be too difficult. I turned up a standard-issue sewing kit, which yielded four needles and a tiny, blunt pair of scissors, and a toolbox, which was functionally worthless. Screwdrivers were nice and all, but Eren's was long and weighted. Too hard to hide. I rolled the scissors up in my sleeve, securing it with two of the needles.

When the couch turned up fistfuls of crumbs and fuzz, I had to revise my image of Eren yet again. Maybe he wasn't the soldier I'd thought he was. Maybe time and despair had changed him into someone else. As hard as it sounded, maybe he really was a stranger.

I glanced around the room. There wouldn't be anything on the screen facing the couch. Too conspicuous, especially if it were repaired. Or monitored. I searched the kitchen, shoving a loaf of bread aside in the process, and found nothing.

I was face-first in the freezer and wrist-deep in the icemaker when the door sucked open, causing me to jump squarely out of my skin.

"Eren."

"This isn't much of a hiding place," he said, his voice gruff. Something in his face made me set my jaw a little tighter. Not regret, exactly. Disappointment, more like. "I don't know what I expected."

No way he didn't have a gun in here somewhere. No way. "Yeah? Give me a minute. I might surprise you."

I slid the door of the icer open and stuck my hand in, never letting my gaze shift from his face. There was something cagey in the way he moved toward me, as though he were anticipating my next move, and I frowned, confused. It was like he was planning something. Preparing for something.

A fight, maybe.

But his face was tired, so tired. His blue eyes met mine at last, and I saw only resignation. I must have imagined his disappointment.

"Are you hungry? I'll make you a sandwich. Grilled cheese." His voice was weary, too.

I backed up. "You stay away from me."

"S'just food, Char."

He came close, and I stepped aside. His face swung near as he reached past my shoulder and lifted a hunk of cheese, then the butter, in the same hand.

The icer door popped shut, and Eren deliberately turned his back to me, setting me off-guard. He wouldn't show me his back if we weren't on the same side. Obviously we weren't going to fight. This was Eren, after all. *My* Eren. I was being ridiculous. Paranoid. Occupational hazard, I supposed.

The nape of his neck had grown pale in the years since we'd left Earth and sunlight, but his haircut hadn't changed—short and blond, no nonsense—and I caught myself staring. Maybe there was a part of me that had missed him for the last five years, even though my mind hadn't.

He whistled tunelessly, setting up a pan and flipping on the burner, but the notes sharpened when he reached for the loaf of bread, causing the hair on my arms to lift up.

The bread.

The bread, the bread.

It was wrapped in a chunky, reusable foil case far too big for a single loaf that crinkled beneath his grip as he pulled it from the shelf.

And it made a dense, muted *thunk* when he laid it on the counter.

When his hand dipped into the package, I swallowed. "Why don't you let me do th—"

Too late. Too late for anything. The gun was suddenly between us, heavy and cold, and my breath froze in my chest.

"Eren."

"You're wanted at headquarters," he said, flicking the stove off.

I'm not sure I understood until that moment what Eren had been to me. How I'd come to think of him, how my mind had relaxed instinctively in his presence. How I'd trusted him. No one had ever made me feel truly secure, like I could believe, cynical as I was, that I would one day be safe for good. Except Eren.

I really was a terrible judge of character.

I wanted to lift my hands in surrender out of habit, but I couldn't make myself do it. It was like admitting that everything was broken, that nothing good would ever last. Which should have been obvious, especially to me, who'd lived through the death of Earth. And my mother.

"I'll never forgive you for this," I said quietly. "In a hundred years, I will not forgive you." I stared at his face, looking for some sign of regret, some indication that my only possible blow had landed true, but the only thing I found was exhaustion. His brow creased for an instant, then everything was smooth. Easy. Done.

"There's nothing for it, Char," he said, almost gently, and any remaining protest died on my lips. "Let's go."

I went. What else could I do?

The hallway stretched before me, gaudy and bright. Maybe Adam would let me wake up in Eirenea, but I doubted it. Maybe, years from now, his horrible drug would become illegal, or he'd die, and I'd be rescued. I'd wake up old, in an old woman's body, with all the experience of a seventeen-year-old failure.

Maybe my family would come for me.

Maybe the years would pass, and my captor would grow lonely, and I'd wake up with children. For ten minutes a year, I'd drink in their faces and worry over the lives they led.

Or maybe he would let me die.

I found my voice halfway to headquarters. "How could you."

29

"It's for the best," he said evenly. "You don't understand. He's too strong."

"He must be, Eren. With you on his side."

"It's not just me. There isn't anyone, on *any* ship, that wants us all to go to war. That's what he's saving us from."

We were a fragile race. We must have always been. Only now, we knew it.

Adam was smug. He had every right to be. I stood before him in the cold room, and he gestured for me to sit. I squared my shoulders and lifted my chin. I wasn't about to spend my last seconds of freedom doing as I was told.

Eventually, his smile grew serious, and my darling husband pressed down on my shoulders until my back hit the chair. The Lieutenant was slouched in a black leather chair nearby. She made no move to assist. Maybe she was drugged, too.

"Welcome back," Adam said brightly. "I know I already said it, but man. It's just so *good* to see the real you, Char."

"We should do this more often," I said.

"Eh, don't hold your breath." His lip twisted around again, and his hand went to his jacket. When I saw the needle, my tongue couldn't swallow, and my throat went numb. "Now, Ambassador," he said. "If you could restrain your wife for a moment."

Eren's hand was warm and heavy on my shoulder, and I chewed the inside of my cheek as hard as I could. The pain was the only good feeling I had left.

Adam rolled his eyes. "You'll have to do better than that. She's awake. That's really her. Take it from me. We can't afford to get complacent."

The Lieutenant stirred, and Eren glanced at her for a moment before crouching down and pulling my arms together behind the chair.

"Now hold still," said Adam. "This'll only sting a bit."

He looked at Eren, who nodded that he was ready, and came close. My arms jerked against Eren's grip involuntarily, and he squeezed them tighter. I went ahead and stopped breathing. I needed to last five more seconds without crying, and I wasn't sure I'd make it.

The needle flashed through the air, taking longer than necessary so that Adam had plenty of time to watch my reaction. I forced every cell in my brain to remain completely frozen. I would not give him the satisfaction. I couldn't. But at the last minute, weakness won, and I closed my eyes.

The pressure on my arms vanished. There was a light *thud*, and my eyes snapped open. The syringe remained secure in Adam's grip, and a wave of mild surprise played over his face. The needle swung in a glinting, silver arc toward me a second time, and as I watched, Eren delivered a second blow, knocking it away.

"Oh," Adam said. "Oh, you're gonna regret that."

"I doubt it," said Eren, his jaw clenched.

"Lieutenant," Adam shouted, "stop him!"

The Lieutenant stood, lumbering, from her chair, but she wasn't much of a soldier. Not anymore. She stumbled toward us, glassy-eyed, and laid into the fight.

So I kicked her.

The top of my foot hit her squarely in the stomach, and she fell backwards, barely affected save for her lack of balance. Adam and the needle were inches away once again. I gripped the seat of my chair with my hand and caught him fully in the chest with my feet, shoving him for all I was worth. But the angle was too high, and my chair skidded back, teetering. Adam kept coming. Eren launched forward at the same time, dangerously close to the needle, and torpedoed into Adam just as my chair lurched back and hit the ground.

I curled up, trying to keep my head from bearing the brunt of the impact, then flipped around as fast as a cat. Syringes are motivating like that.

But the fight was over. Eren was faster, stronger, and better trained. Adam made a move to stab him with the needle, but Eren used the movement to secure a grip on Adam's exposed wrist. I lost sight of the needle for a moment, but Eren pulled himself up and landed a knee on Adam's throat, pinning him. Without releasing his grip, he calmly removed the syringe from Adam's clenched fist and slid it into his upper arm.

Eren tossed the syringe away and maintained his position while waiting for the drug to take effect. They locked eyes until Adam's angry, grunting pant dissolved into a helpless growl. Finally, his eyes glassed over, and his struggle ended.

The Lieutenant was sitting, half-reclined, on the ground near a chair. She didn't look to be much of a threat anymore, either.

Eren stood, straightened his uniform, and looked at me. "You okay?"

I gaped at him.

"I'm sorry I couldn't tell you," he said gently, taking a step toward me. "He watches—"

"Back *up*," I said. "You stay away from me."

He stopped in an instant, like someone had slammed a door an inch from his nose. "Charlotte. You have to understand—"

"What? That Adam was watching you? And that's why you just had to let him keep me in stasis for *five years*? That's why you had to bring me back here to him?"

He swallowed, sorting his words before he spoke them out in a slow, careful string. "I was trying to protect you."

"Yeah," I said, my voice breaking. He stepped toward me, and I backed away. I lifted my hand, and again, he stopped.

A moment passed, and he took a seat in the chair, defeated. "Charlotte, please. I didn't have a choice."

"Right."

"He was following us the whole time. Every single word. *I'm wearing a k-band*, for goodness'— He can literally hear everything I do, and he knows when I'm lying. Look. I was so afraid he'd hurt you if he ever suspected me. I had to be completely sure you'd broken out before I could even *think* about..." Eren trailed off. "I had to fool you *both*. I practically had to fool myself. It was the only way to keep you safe. If I'd been wrong about you, or if he'd figured it out—"

"I just spent five years trapped in my own head," I said, my voice hard. "With no control over what he did to me, or what he made me do. But it's good to hear how safe I was that whole time."

Some tiny, near-dead part of my mind knew that my anger was misplaced, at least in part, but the gray madness of Adam's prison had pushed it so far down I couldn't reach it. I was finally coherent, and my rage built to an apex.

I wanted Adam dead.

I wanted Eren *gone*.

I wanted to fly so far away that I never saw any of them, including this cursed ship, ever again.

I wanted my mom.

I was so caught up in the injustice of everything, in the newness of my mind's freedom, that I didn't see the shadow moving just outside my vision until it had grown too large to stop. "*Er*—" I began, but my word was cut short by a strangling pressure around my throat. Adam's fingers were cold, but he was very much awake. His nails were barely longer than what could pass as normal, and they bit into the skin, like he was making a fist instead of just squeezing. He did not look me in the eye.

"Char!" Eren shouted, too late. He sprang from the chair, but the Lieutenant's lumbering form was faster. I braced myself, preparing to fight her, too, but the world was already going dark. At the last moment, just as she was about to hit me, her body juddered and swung to one side.

I had the strange sensation that time had slowed, and I struggled to watch as she slammed instead into Adam. A strong jerk shook my vision as she delivered him another blow, and his grip on my neck finally loosened.

And then Eren was there, shoving her aside and hitting Adam so hard that he sprawled onto the ground next to me. I choked in some air and tried to stand. I couldn't.

A few feet away, the Lieutenant's slow gaze turned from me to Adam, and together, we watched him fade. Eren stood over his body, fists tight, and turned to look down at me.

"She—" I tried to speak, but was wracked by a cough.

"Lieutenant?" Eren said.

She looked at him mildly, like a puppy preparing for a nap. "Where am I?" she said.

"In headquarters," said Eren. "You're in stasis, mostly. I think."

"Unlike Adam," I said. "He has some kind of immunity?"

But instead of answering, the Lieutenant slumped to the floor. "I wasn't always..." she said, and closed her eyes.

As I watched her, the knot in my chest doubled down,

pulling tighter. Maybe Eren was right, and we were all just Adam's prisoners.

But I was still out of breath and exceedingly unwilling to think about Eren right then. I knew the feeling that crept through me, and I hated it. It had only ever made me weak.

Eren, meanwhile, wasted no time in shoving a chair into the doorframe. Grunting, he slung Adam into another chair and cuffed his hands through the armrest. By the time he finished that, I moved to search Adam's jacket. When I came near, Eren stepped away.

"No antidote," he said. "He doesn't keep it on him." I didn't answer, and he shifted awkwardly back to help the Lieutenant, his mouth tight. About the ti—me he got her into a comfortable-looking position, I found Adam's holster.

He was armed, of course, but I didn't recognize the weapon. It was some kind of oblong metal box that came to a point at one end. One side had a flip-button labeled with letters etched into the metal by hand. "$D F^- DEW...$" I looked up. "What the heck does that mean?"

Eren looked at the weapon, avoiding my eyes. "Deuterium Fluoride Directed Energy Weapon. I've actually seen that one in action. It concentrates a stream of infrared chemicals—heavy hydrogen, for example—and neutralizes the target via plasma breakdown."

"Plasma..." I muttered. "Hang on. Are you telling me he made a real-life laser gun?"

"Yeah," said Eren. "Pet project of his."

"Aren't they all." I turned it in my hand, thinking, and aimed it at Adam's head. "So let's see how he did." My thumb hadn't quite caught the flip when Eren knocked into me, throwing the blaster into a wall.

Speechless, I watched it fall before turning back to Eren

to stare a death-ray of my own straight into his face, which was inches from mine. "You have got to be kidding me right now."

"Charlotte. You can't kill him." He had the tone of a man trying to talk a cat down from a tree, but there was a sense of urgency he was trying to subdue. So maybe the cat was dangerous, like a lion. Or maybe the tree was on fire.

Either way, I found it annoying.

"Eren, *get off me*. And let's test that theory, shall we? Move." I shoved him as hard as I could manage, and he moved back a fraction of an inch, mostly out of courtesy.

I leaned over, reaching for the blaster, and he caught me by the wrist again. His voice remained soft, in sharp contrast to mine. "Listen, you can't. Life support is wired to his vitals. If he dies, we all do."

He paused, watching me. When he was sure his words had sunk in, his grip relaxed.

A moment later, I let some of the tension fall from my own stance. "Okay. Let me go," I said, more calmly. "All the way."

He backed up, looking pained, and took a seat in the chair again. His shoulders slumped a little, and he leaned forward, looking up at me from a much lower vantage point. It was about as non-threatening a stance as any I'd seen. He still made me nervous.

"Sorry," I said quietly.

He nodded. "Me too."

"Can we switch it to someone else's vitals? Maybe someone can hack in."

He shook his head. "The system is keyed to his heartbeat. No one can replicate that."

Adam was always a step ahead. "We'll never be safe while he's alive, Eren," I said.

Eren didn't hear me. "So how did he attack you? Not that it matters, but shouldn't he have been more like a puppet?"

I shook my head. "He wasn't in stasis. That's for sure. You can't make decisions in stasis. You can remember feelings, like fear or sorrow, but nothing concrete, like needing to attack someone."

"The Lieutenant would beg to differ," Eren said dryly.

"I don't know how she did that, either. Adam must have some kind of automatic antidote. Or he saved the heavy doses just for me. Or he's engineered a formula that only he's immune to," I mused. "There's no telling. Anyway, he's definitely out now."

Eren nodded, staring at the floor, the wall, Adam's sleeping form, and finally, me. "Good. Because there's something I need to tell you."

# Five

Eren yanked a stick-like gadget from Adam's jacket and turned to the comm panel. I'd seen it once before, when Adam had used it to steal an Arkhopper. The panel hummed to life, and Eren pulled the comm device toward his mouth, keying a code into the board. A moment later, it lit up. "Everest to Tribune. Come in, Turner."

I stood straight, electrified.

Eren looked back at me and grinned. I continued to gape until my voice bubbled up, and suddenly, I was shouting. "Dad? Dad, are you there?!"

Eren held up a hand to quiet me.

"You," I hissed at him. "I have questions for you."

"He's been in touch a few times a year. Keeps this line open. But he couldn't get to you. Adam's always watching."

"And you decided to keep it a *secret*? Of course you did. Dad! Where are you!"

"We were *trying* to *protect* you, Charlotte. Just until we could get you out. And believe me, we have tried everything. It's more complicated than you realize. We tried getting to *her*," he nodded toward the Lieutenant, "but Adam must have kept her on a tight leash." He shook his head a little.

"We figured she was loyal to him. We tried constructing our own antidote, but he just changed the formula. Nothing ever worked."

The comm popped, and my father's voice filled the room. It was intensely familiar, unchanged in the five years since I'd heard it. "Turner to Tribune Liaison. What's the news, Eren?"

"Dad!" I shouted. "Where are you?"

There was a pause, then my father made a sound I couldn't identify. "Charlotte," he said slowly. "Eren, is that—is she—?"

"She's out of stasis," said Eren. "And Adam's down. For now."

"Dad! Where are you?" I repeated. "Did you make it to Europe?"

"I'm here, Charlotte. I never left."

"But, *how?*"

"I called in every favor I had," he said. "Every last one. That's the short version, anyway."

He sounded like there was more to say, but Eren interrupted. "Sir, we need to move. We have to assume that Adam set traps. There's no time."

"I'm ready," my father answered. "Meet me at the dock in ten minutes sharp. Don't be late." There was a pause, and another sound, this one like a half-laugh. "Charlotte. Welcome back. It's good to hear your voice again. It really is."

"You too, Dad," I said. "We'll be right there."

"Turner out," he said, and the mic turned black again.

I stared at the empty panel. My father was alive. We were going to be together. I took a deep breath.

*My father hadn't left me.*

I angled toward the door, catching Eren's eye. "Let's go."

"Yeah," he said slowly. "We should go."

I followed his frowning gaze to the Lieutenant. She was peacefully asleep, mere feet away from the most dangerous person I'd ever known. "I mean, it's not the worst idea, you know? Leaving. Escaping. Staying alive." I bit a lip. After all, she had chosen to work for Adam, hadn't she?

"We have no antidote," Eren said. "She's gonna stay in stasis until he comes around. Although, he *is* tied up."

"I guarantee that's not gonna hold him once he's awake. We could try to give her someplace to hide."

"There is no hiding on this ship, Char." Eren sounded irritated. "Certainly not on the Guardian Level. Besides, she's barely conscious."

"She'll slow us down," I said, but Eren just stood there, waiting.

Finally, I sighed. "You're not going to leave her, are you." It wasn't a question.

He shook his head.

I smiled in spite of myself. Maybe he hadn't changed as much as I'd thought.

"You get this side," he said, putting her left arm around my shoulders. He ducked to lift her the rest of the way to her feet. "Perhaps it won't be so bad."

I stood, supporting her. "Or perhaps she was acting on some kind of stasis-induced hallucination, and as soon as she snaps out of it, she'll kill us all."

"Ever the optimist." He returned the smile. "Let's go. Watch the doorframe."

But something held me back. I stood there for a moment, trying to think, then slowly let go of her arm. "Hang on. We need a better plan."

"How did you put it? Escaping? Staying alive? This is a *very good plan*." Eren made a face from the hallway. "Brilliant, even."

"No, it leaves us open. We need protection, Eren."

"Char—" he said softly.

"Here's the thing. If we take her—" I waved at the Lieutenant—"we save one person. It's the wrong play."

Eren looked from corridor, to me, to Adam's chair. "Oh, no you don't. Now *that* is a bad plan."

"Hear me out," I said hastily. "We can't kill him. Not yet. And he controls everything on this Ark. So we can't lock him up. Not here. It's the right move, Eren. It's checkmate."

"No, it's stalemate at best. It's nuts, is what it is. Do you have any idea how strong he is?"

I swallowed. "None of us does. That's the problem."

I waited while he considered that. A moment passed, and he laid the Lieutenant down with a pointed sigh.

"Good. You get that side," I said, popping the cuffs off Adam's wrists and shoving them into my pocket. As soon as they clicked open, Eren was at my side, ready to fight again. But Adam didn't move. I pulled his arm over my shoulder.

"This is insane." He made an angry grunt and hefted Adam's remaining weight off the chair.

"Your objection is noted," I said cheerfully. It was about time we got the upper hand around here. "Come on. Let's do this."

We stumbled into the dock with about a minute to spare. "Dad?" I called around the room in a half-whisper. I had never taken the Guardian entrance to the hangar before. It was imposing even when sealed shut. I turned to Eren. "You got the control stick-thingy?"

"Yes." Eren looked around. "Did you feel that?"

"Feel what? Do you think he's on the other side already?"

"Your dad? No. He couldn't be. He's got the skins—the suits. I think the Ark just moved."

"It's your imagination," I said. Eren looked pale. Well, paler than usual. "The skins?"

"They never repaired the seal in the hangar. Without skins, we die."

I swallowed against the dizzying feeling that the only thing separating me from the vast vacuum of space was a sheet of glass. "Dad!"

"Hey, keep it down. He has ears everywhere." Eren laid a hand on the window, as though steadying himself, and laid his half of Adam gently on the floor. He looked sick.

I nodded. "Yeah, but be careful with the glass, okay? I'm not looking to take the quick way out."

Eren stared down at Adam's limp form, then looked back at me. "It's fused silica," he said.

What did that have to do with anything? "Silica. Great. Congrats on reading the pre-flight materials."

Eren made a face like he wanted to laugh, but couldn't, and slid down to sit next to Adam. "Fused. With titanium, too. Like the k-bands." He waved a wrist at me, and his kuang band glinted in the bright light coming from the hangar. He had a strange look on his face.

"Hey. You okay?"

He looked down. "Char. I'm sorry." His hand closed around the metal band on his wrist, and it hit me that he'd been wearing it for the last five years. I guess life hadn't been so great for either of us.

"For what? Hey, get up. You're kinda scaring me. Eren. We gotta find my dad."

"Sorry it took five years. Sorry I couldn't get you out of this any sooner." He slumped forward. "No matter what, you leave. Don't stay here." His forehead touched the concrete, and his shoulders relaxed.

"Eren. *Eren.* Get up. Please get up. Wake up." I shook him as hard as I could, but he only flopped onto his back, eyes closed.

"Charlotte?"

The sound jolted through me, and I whirled around. "Dad? Help! He's—"

My father came running out of a shadow, and I had the absurd thought that exactly ten minutes had passed since our conversation. To the second.

He pressed a hand into Eren's neck. "He's breathing. Pulse is—fine, probably. Put this on," he said, shoving a skin into my arms.

I wasted no time in getting the rubbery material over Eren's feet. "I'm gonna need help lifting up his hips."

Dad was glancing around the ceiling, a gesture that seemed out of place for him. I'd never really seen my dad get nervous. "No, Charlotte. Not on him. On *you.* Hurry up."

My lips froze, mouth open, and I took a second to steel my spine. "I'm not leaving him," I said quietly.

"It was always the plan. He has to stay here, Charlotte. There's a chip in his k-band."

"Then it doesn't matter whether he stays here or not. He's…" I trailed off, unable to finish the thought aloud. *He's dead either way.*

Dad chose that moment to wrap an arm around my shoulder, a second gesture I couldn't quite place with him, and squeeze.

I returned the embrace, surprised. We hadn't hugged much during our last few years on Earth. He added his other arm, and for the moment, I had the irrepressible feeling that things would be okay. That no matter what, my problems were no match for my dad.

His eyes traveled down my right arm, to the place where my wrist should have been, and he hesitated before speaking. "I know. I know. But Eren knew the risks. He was very clear."

"Are you worried about being spied on? We'll just wrap the band up with aluminum, like you did mine."

"It's worse than spying, Charlotte. He's been drugged. He could easily be dead before we get him on the Arkhopper."

I shook my head, frustrated. No way was Adam going to win this one. "How many skins did you bring?"

"Two."

"Two." I said, hopping up. "So we need two more." I trotted around the area, tapping on wall panels. A few held emergency supplies, including a military-grade first-aid kit, which I ignored, and a pressurized flare gun, which I grabbed out of habit.

"Charlotte—" he said gently.

"We can't leave Eren. And we sure can't leave Adam. So two more skins."

His eyes widened. "*That's Adam?* Charlotte."

I whirled around, halfway to the other side of the hangar door, and filled my voice with lead. "Dad. I am not leaving them."

"Well, we're not staying here. I can't let you—" Dad stopped, recognizing my tone, and gritted his teeth. Then he took a breath, regarding me with a measure of thoughtfulness. "I suppose it does give us some leverage."

"Right?" I breathed a sigh of relief. At least one person didn't think my plan was insane. I returned to my search, whacking the next panel I came to. The compartment opened to reveal one skin. One.

It was better than nothing. I lifted my chin and knocked open the rest of the panels, but it seemed that Adam had stored only enough for himself.

I turned back to Dad. "Okay. Three skins. Not ideal."

Dad shook his head. I slid down next to Eren and began to work the skin over his boots again. "How far from here to the bay?"

"Ten feet, maybe? It's the first ship in the hangar. Only ship, actually."

"And Adam hasn't disabled it?"

"We think it's his getaway vehicle. I'm sure he's got some trick or another up his sleeve in case someone else takes off with it. But he's in stasis, right?"

My hand had wandered to the back of Eren's head, and I pulled it away as casually as I could before my dad noticed. "Nope. Good old-fashioned knockout."

Dad nodded. "That works, too," he said slowly.

Too slowly.

He laid a hand over mine, and I stopped trying to secure the skin on Eren's hips.

"What?" I said impatiently.

He gave me a slow look. "Charlotte."

"*What?*"

"We have three skins."

"I know."

"We can't leave Adam. You and I are agreed on that point."

45

I pulled Eren's head onto my legs without really thinking about it. It filled my entire lap. His face was completely relaxed. He was so helpless, in spite of his size. In that moment, there was no one but me to protect him. "I'm *not* leaving Eren. He never left me."

"Eren's unconscious, sweetheart. He can't fly the hopper." He lowered his voice. "You need to understand. There's so much we don't know about stasis. He may not wake up."

"I'm not leaving him," I repeated stubbornly. "I'm taking him to the doctors over there. Who knows what Adam's done to him?"

It occurred to me that my father was as strong-willed as I'd ever been. At least I got it honestly. "Charlotte," he said gently. "One skin for you. One for me, to fly the ship. And one..."

I pursed my lips, understanding his point at last. "For Adam. Because if he dies in the vacuum, we all do."

Dad nodded.

"So take *them*. I'm the only one you don't need. And I'll be fine. No k-band or anything."

"I won't do that, Charlotte. Whatever you think you're capable of, you're not safe here. I'm not leaving you again." His voice took on its own kind of strength—not anger, as I'd heard in the past, but something closer to resolution. "That's the deal. Either you come with me, or no one does. Besides," he smiled strangely, "if Adam didn't kill me, Eren would."

"So maybe we're not going anywhere, after all," I said. Stalemate again.

Dad looked at me, then back to the wall. "What do you want, Charlotte?"

"What do you mean?"

"What is it that you want? You've been fighting against things all your life. What are you fighting *for* these days?"

"I want—" I stopped, thinking. "I want my family back. I want the ships to be safe. All of them." I took another long pause and leveled my gaze with his. "And I want Adam dead."

"Then we have to get on that hopper. We have no allies here. This entire Ark is rigged to kill dissenters. Anyone who stands up to him. That's why he's lasted so long." There was a change in his tone. "And your brother is on the European Ark."

"Then Eren is no safer here than anyone else. Even if we leave him."

He looked out the window. "Once the door is open, that's it. The air will be sucked out of the area. Our intelligence is that the seal to this door will blow. A secondary seal will engage around the loading dock. He did that in some other areas so that he couldn't be followed. This entire room will likely become a vacuum. There may be other tricks as well."

"I don't doubt it," I said. "But I'm not leaving Eren."

We sat there another moment, at a total impasse, and bit by bit, the absurdity of the situation crept over me. I had to laugh.

Dad smiled, too, friendly but humorless. "We really are stuck, aren't we? We make quite a pair."

I shook my head. "There's nothing I could say to get you to take him to the doctor for me."

"Nope," he said flatly. "And I don't suppose I could persuade you to—"

"Nope."

At this, he laughed, too. "Well, there is one other option. But you're not going to like it."

47

# Six

"All right," I said. "Let's hear it."

"It's ten feet to the hopper. It'll take at least fifteen seconds to pop the hatch, then another thirty to seal it back."

I gave him a blank look. "Dad. You can't be seriously thinking of—"

"You hold his face, keep pressure on his eyes. Make sure his mouth and nose are shut."

"Dad. No. *No.*"

"I'll run ahead and get it ready. There's still full gravity, and we should keep him in the fetal position as long as possible. As soon as it starts to open, I'll be right back to help you move him."

"You have actually lost your—"

He looked at me earnestly. "Even a dog can survive ninety seconds. A chimp can make it for two and a half minutes."

"I do not want to think about how they figured that one out."

"It's certainly not safe, but like you said. The scientists on the EuroArk have been working around the clock on reproducing these drugs ever since Adam took over. They can probably help Eren. And I doubt he's going to make it if we leave him here."

"So put the skin on *him*. I'm not even slightly sick. My odds are way better."

"That won't work, Charlotte, even if I agreed to it. I can't move three bodies by myself. And you will concede that Adam's life is more important than any of ours. We can't risk him."

"For now, anyway." I sat there, fully confronted with the truth: my father was right. It had to be Eren. "I can't believe I'm agreeing to this."

"It's his best shot." He paused for a moment, then added, "You're a good friend to him, Charlotte. I'm proud of you."

"All right, all right." I stood up and shimmied into my skin, yanking it nervously over my shoulders. The flat oxygen pack settled around the top of my head, under the dome of my helmet, and the neck sealed itself without a hitch. Beside me, Dad did the same, then started working on Adam.

I popped back to the first-aid kit and retrieved a spool of surgical tape. Then I wound it around Eren's mouth about a dozen times, making sure he was still breathing through his nose. I plugged his ears with skinwax from the burn section of the kit and taped his eyelids shut, then wrapped them tightly as well. Halfway through, I realized that my hands were shaking.

"Ninety seconds, you say?"

Dad gave me a sympathetic look. "More, for a person."

"A conscious one." My tongue felt heavy. "Forty-five seconds for the hatch to open and close."

"Plus a little time to get Adam on board. And however long it takes for life support to boot."

"I think I'm going to be sick."

49

Dad looked at Eren, and I realized I was cradling his head and shoulders against my chest. "I don't want him to die any more than you do, Charlotte," he said, his voice slightly softer.

I pulled Eren closer. He was completely limp. "Yeah."

"Did you see any rope?"

"Rope?"

"In the compartments."

"Um. Yeah. Somewhere on that side."

Moving quickly, Dad located the rope, produced a knife out of nowhere, and cut a long measure off. Then he wound it around Adam's chest and over my shoulders. "You should take Adam," he said, his voice strange. "We'll move faster. I'll hold Eren in position, with his knees up. He's bigger. Less secure. It'll take a lot more strength."

I nodded, numb, and he secured Adam's body onto my back, then wound his legs around my waist. "Hang on like this," he said quietly. "It'll distribute around your hips. Easier to manage."

I wet my lips. "Okay."

"Okay," he repeated, lifting Eren against his chest. He rested a hand on the door to the hangar. "When this is open, the pressure differential will activate the airlock on the far side of the hangar. We think it's wired so that the airlock's activation will trigger an explosion, so move fast. Brace yourself. In five."

Eren was curled against my father like a baby. His head was tucked against my father's neck, his shins against my father's forearm. I nodded.

"Four. Three. Two—"

There was a sick *hiss* as the distant airlock engaged its seal. I lumbered out onto the hangar catwalk, Adam on my back, following my father's heavy-laden form. Behind us, the door began to close.

Seconds later, a gut-thumping *POP* followed by a deep, sudden rumble shook the hangar floor, and the walls around me reflected fire. At the hangar wall, mere feet from the dock, a bright orange flame came into view and quickly flattened into a deep, dark blue as the fire devoured the remaining oxygen trying to escape the hangar.

I stumbled, falling, and let go of Adam's legs. The rope around us both went dangerously taut, driving my breath out of my chest. I hit the ground, and Adam's weight thrust me down further, smashing my knees into the floor. The hopper was round and shiny, with a webbed net over half the hatch and long, black blades that looked like the feet of a particularly graceful insect.

It was also about a million miles away. I struggled to stand, but my legs were not nearly strong enough to lift us both after five years of puppethood, and I had to crawl the remaining distance.

When the ladder appeared in front of my face, I lifted my head in time to see my father force Eren through the hatch. I grabbed the highest rung I could reach and yanked myself up. Dad leaned down and pulled Adam up. He was still attached to me.

Surely an hour had passed since the seal had broken.

I willed my legs and arms to climb the ladder, then collapsed onto Eren as soon as I'd struggled over the lid of the hopper.

Above me, the hatch must have closed, but I couldn't hear it. The floor of the hopper began to hum.

My father sat in the pilot seat, yanking the controls around, until the hatch was fully sealed. Then he ripped off his helmet and shoved it down over Eren's head, flipping a dial on the ear.

"What?" I said, but he couldn't hear me. I yanked off my own helmet and breathed in the recycled air of the hopper, nearly shaking with relief. "What is it?"

"Nothing," said Dad. "He's fine, probably. But the oxygen in the helmet is more concentrated. That's what he needs right now, since we can hardly repressurize him slowly. Anything he had in his blood is likely depleted, or will be soon."

"Oh," I said, then drew it out a little longer, feeling fear and relief all at once. "Ohhh."

Dad frowned at me, then shoved an airsick tube into my unsteady hands. "Make sure if you vomit, you get it all in *that*," he said crisply, and began to cut the ropes off my back. Adam fell onto the footboard, and his helmeted head knocked into Eren's.

There were only two seats in the hopper: the pilot's and the one right next to it. So I went about pressing Eren into a sitting position on the floor. From there, I could try to lift him onto the seat using the safety straps as leverage. If memory served, we were in for a spin once we broke free of the Ark's rotation, and I wasn't about to risk him getting hurt any further. If Adam suffered a few broken bones, on the other hand, I wouldn't exactly lose sleep over it.

"Charlotte. The seat is yours," my father said. He was gathering the bits of rope from around my shoulders and using them to bind Adam in every way he could think of. Then he pulled Eren down on top of Adam and tied their chests together. "This will keep them from snapping their necks, but only barely. It won't work as well for you."

"Eren goes in the seat," I said, angry. "He has more mass. He should be secured. For everyone's safety."

"I'm done with this argument, Charlotte. Buckle in."

I set my lips, weighing my options.

Dad sighed. "I'm securing them both to the floorboard. No one's going flying around the cabin. And if you don't buckle up, no one's going anywhere." He crossed his arms and settled back in his seat. "Unless you've learned how to fly a spacecraft since we left Earth."

I scowled. He looked out the window, the picture of patience. The flames had long since extinguished from lack of oxygen, and the hopper was like a cocoon, quiet and safe. And slightly cramped. My father wasn't kidding.

I hopped into the seat, letting my glare deepen a little further, and grimaced my way through the process of untangling and securing the knot of safety straps. Dad gave a slight nod and shifted the controls into position.

The thrusters engaged when the final valve released, stabilizing us as we swung out into the darkness. Gravity lessened with every sweeping arc, and we slid smoothly into nothingness, surrounded by distant stars. Dad was a better pilot than I'd expected.

I let the vastness envelop me completely. For the first time, I felt that space was comforting. We—all of us—were so helpless. There was no rational explanation for our continued survival in the universe, and yet here we were, blanketed by the cosmos that should have killed us off generations ago.

It struck me that if we succeeded, we would be the forbears of a new race of people. In time, the generations we carried inside ourselves would come to fill Eirenea, and it was we who made their strivings possible. We who had escaped a doomed planet. We who founded a life on a barren rock on the other side of the solar system. They would teach the story of our journey for the rest of our existence. And who knew what things the human race would yet accomplish?

I glanced at my dad and knew that his mind was on the past, and my mother. For me, in that moment, it was all connected. She had given her life so that I could be here, and now, I was prepared to do the same.

"We're going to make it, Dad. I think she always knew that we would make it."

He said nothing, but spun the ship about and pressed us into the void.

# Seven

The EuroArk was dark when we came in. I'm not sure what I expected, but the only major points of light were the docks. There were tiny pins of light at the tips of the other structures, but I couldn't make them out. I squinted, slack-jawed, as we drew near. I couldn't imagine the shape of the massive ship ahead of me. From where I sat, it looked exactly like the stars.

"Gotta be careful here," said Dad, mostly to himself. "The cities reach farther out than the docks."

I continued to gawk, wondering what he meant by that, until the rest of the Ark came to light. It was a dark ship in a darker sky, but from what I could tell, it was composed of several cube-like modules connected by a series of wide tubes and interspersed with smaller, more tapered tubes that held the docks.

"It looks like a jack," I said, recalling a game I'd played as a child. "Knucklebones."

"Yes, that was intentional, to preserve and insulate as many cultures as possible. So is the darkness. It's mandatory for eight hours a night. Saves energy. Helps with the Lightness, too. Gets people used to power outages before they happen."

The hopper eased toward the space between a protruding pair of cities, allowing me to gape at the vacant-looking windows in wonder. "They don't have a nuclear generator? I hope you got your clearance ahead of time," I said nervously, looking for weapons ports among the asteroid shields. "What do you mean, intentional?"

"The European Ark was engineered to minimize interdependency among the cities. The areas at the end of each strut operate separately, but the core city, right in the middle, has final say over everything. Kinda like the United States, before it was dissolved. And it adds surface area for the solar sails."

"Minimize inter—but wait, isn't the whole point of the Treaty of Phoenix that we're all supposed to depend on each other? To stop everyone from going to war again? We're all mixed together, so that no one group of people gets isolated. I gotta wonder what the Tribune thinks about that. It has the final say over everything, right?"

"That's an untested theory, at this point. The Tribune has never done anything controversial enough to matter, so no one has ever challenged its authority. But it's really meant to arbitrate disputes under the Treaty. It's more of a legal recourse for the heads of the governments than an executive one. Its only weight is the strength of the other Arks, who've all agreed to abide by its rulings."

"In theory."

"In theory," he nodded. "But if they could be persuaded to side with an ally instead... who knows what would happen."

I didn't see the point of an all-powerful Tribune that had no actual power. "But we've been in space for more than five years. Surely they've noticed that Adam's broken a few rules by now."

"No one has formally challenged him yet, so the Tribune hasn't had a chance to declare him illegitimate. Look. When we left Earth, it sounded like the right plan. But it's not like the Tribune has weapons, or an army, unlike everyone else, apparently. No teeth, no power. And again, no one's ever challenged Adam."

I grimaced. "So they're scared. So he's got no one to stop him."

"It's not like they *like* him. But he's been pretty clear about his terms for peace: back off. Look the other way, and you can sleep safe in your beds at night. He won't come after you. And it's not like the other Arks really want the Tribune getting involved, anyway. The Asian Ark is in the same situation, with total power consolidated in a single person."

"An," I said, thinking of the pale, regal Imperial of the Asian Ark, who'd forced me to marry Eren, the son of our enemy, and jettison our nukes in a futile attempt to stave off a civil war on the North American Ark. The difference between An and Adam, though, was that Adam had seized power through his brilliant technological capabilities, and An had probably been chosen to lead her Ark before we ever left Earth.

"They're both strong enough to make the other Arks toe the line. It's impossible not to believe their threats," said Dad.

"Well," I said dryly, "something tells me they'll be a lot more willing to support our return to democracy when we deliver him straight to them."

"I do like our odds," he agreed, totally focused on the port directly in front of us. "Depressurize the docking latches."

I looked at him blankly.

"The landing gear," he said, gesturing at the far end of the panel.

"Um."

"That yellow switch-thingy right in front of you. Flip it. Qui—you know what, I got it." He unbuckled a couple of straps, fingers flying, and yanked off his head restraints. Then he leaned across me to pop a lever. "There."

"Oh, riiiight. The docking latches," I muttered. "They were still *pressurized*."

He laughed, an unusual response for him, and looked thoughtful. "I could teach you to fly it, you know. Sometime."

That was the last thing on earth I expected him to say. I focused on the deck ahead, too surprised to look at him. "Yeah, Dad. Sometime."

I flipped open as many restraints as I could while the tiny hangar pressurized around us. Like the dock in the North American Ark, this one was built in what was basically the center hold of a massive airlock, with a pressurized seal on either side. Unlike our hangar, this one was designed to receive no more than two hoppers at a time. Its walls and floor were deep blue, and the porthole on the door to the inner seal was much smaller, but I could still see straight into the receiving chamber on the other side of the door from my elevated seat in the hopper. By the time we had the all-clear to pop the hopper's forward hatch, I had moved on to slicing through the ropes around Eren and Adam.

I didn't realize I was moving unsteadily until I found Eren's pulse and my arms suddenly stopped shaking. I slid to the floor panel to hold his head against me. He was breathing. His face was still bandaged, and I felt a wave of nerves at the thought of unsticking his ears or eyes just yet. It was silly, though. It's not like our safety was guaranteed in the inner parts of the Ark, either, but I left his wrappings where they were.

"Mr. Turner, sir?"

"Thanks, Jax. We've brought some cargo, as I mentioned in my transmission."

"Yes, sir."

Jax leaped up the side of the hopper. If he was surprised that the "cargo" was human, he hid it well. A quick check of Adam's vitals, and he began distributing orders to a skeleton crew on the ground.

My father helped lift Eren into the arms of a waiting crewman, then we both hopped to the ground. "You'll want to take extra care with that one," he said, indicating Adam. "He's out, but he's dangerous. In fact, if we could spare a second to speak with the director on board, that might be best."

Jax tossed a comm device at my father, who plugged it into his ear and began a discreet conversation under the wing of a nearby ship. I glanced around the hangar. It was small but full to bursting, and I smiled.

It was nice to be on a ship that hadn't succumbed to Adam's swath of destruction.

Were these men part of the Tribune's forces, or were they here on behalf of the European leadership? I was just starting to question the legality of our presence when the nearest crew member leaned over Eren, then motioned for her companions to assist in lifting him. "He's all right?" she asked.

"Yeah, I think so," said another. "We ought to get him to a doctor as soon as possible, though."

"Okay," Dad interrupted hurriedly, returning the comm device. "I'm officially surrendering this—*man*—to the authority of the European Ark. The orders are to restrain him as closely as possible, like I said, but we should move fast. I'll rest easy once he's in a cell."

The group exchanged a quick glance of curiosity, but they were happy to comply, and we headed toward the second door of the airlock at a brisk pace. My heart rate sped up, and I realized Dad was acting a little nervous. He and I were separated by a few people, all of whom leaned in, consciously or not, to be sure they caught everything he said. It was a familiar sight in a strange setting.

Two men carried Eren, and a couple more crew members had Adam, including the woman who'd spoken to me.

"I'm not sure," my dad was saying, and his voice suddenly carried to the back of the group. "You'd have to ask my daughter. Charlotte, what's the story on the drug Adam's been using? They're going to need a complete rundown of everything you know. Size, color, dosage, whatever methods he uses to adminis—"

A high-pitched scream erupted from behind me, followed immediately by a light thud. I jerked around to see one of the crew members on the ground, unconscious.

Oh, no. *No, no, no.*

Adam stood, unsupported, in the middle of our group, a long, black stick dangling from his grip. It wasn't a stunner—it was more narrow than that—and my grip tightened on my helmet. I couldn't see his sinister grin through the mask on his helmet, but I knew it was there.

"Dad, *run!*" I shouted, and jumped toward Eren. He was half-supported by his remaining crew member, but I was too late. Adam broke off the handle of the stick and threw it into the floor between us. It landed like a gummy, weighted puck and began to smoke. My brain clouded with terror.

What horrors had we brought to this Ark?

Two of the crew tried to tackle him. I wanted to scream at them to stay away, but my mouth felt fuzzy. Everyone who made contact with his stick was immediately thrown back, unconscious.

The smoke grew thicker and began to fizz.

"Charlotte!" my father yelled, and I reached for Eren. In the same moment, the panel beneath the puck gave way as the puck melted through the bottom of the hangar. There was a sickening *hiss* as the hull was breached and the airlock gave up its seal.

I slammed my helmet over the gaping hole and, holding it down with my bad arm, pressed my hand around the loose elastic of its neck so hard my wrist ached immediately. I couldn't tell whether my makeshift seal was effective until I heard a rubbery sucking noise that stopped when I spread my fingers a bit wider around the collar.

That's when I finally heard someone calling my name, clipped and distorted in a familiar, sickening tone. *Char.* Like something burning.

Adam came near me, stick extended, and too late, I opened my mouth to scream. My neck went cold where the stick touched it, but he didn't pull the trigger. His face came near to mine, and I contemplated yanking the helmet off the hole it protected.

I could kill him, right here.

He would take me with him, of course. That was an acceptable price to pay. But the vacuum would claim Eren and my father, and Adam's death would end my Ark, so I forced my hand to remain where it was.

He didn't touch me. Instead, he laid a hand on the helmet, toying with the seal and watching my panicked reaction with interest. His gaze broke only for a moment as he assessed the progress of the EuroArk's response.

"Come and find me, Char. I'll be waiting for you at the end of the storm. So come and find me."

His arm twitched as he activated the weapon at my neck, and my face hit the panel. He lifted the smallest part of the neck flap a fraction of an inch, breaking the seal, and I breathed out the air that the vacuum claimed as the hangar blanked out of view.

Through his mask, I thought I heard Adam laughing.

# Eight

*I am lying on the couch, face up, staring at the ceiling in my parents' den. Our den. It's warm. I am safe.*

*I've been out of juvy for three days. My parents are still tiptoeing around me, not asking any pointed questions about my latest stint, but West and I, we've had a lot to catch up on. And this time, I'm doing everything right. They didn't have to take my phone away—I gave it to them. When the psych stopped by, I didn't hold back. My caseworker brought me a doughnut, and I listened to everything he said. We signed me up for some classes online. I'm already three lectures in, and that was only yesterday! All physics, though. You got to stick to your strengths.*

*I don't like sleeping in my room. Too isolated. But Mom and Dad don't say a word when I park it on the couch my first night home. I've barely moved since. Just a few trips to West's room when the parents are asleep. Mom even kissed my forehead before she left for work last night. I grin at the ceiling fan. It's almost like anything is possible.*

*All in all, these are maybe the best three days of my life. I have the house to myself right now, and all I want to do*

63

*is sleep. And eat, obviously. Later, I'll knock out a few more classes. Maybe even tackle English lit. Maybe.*

*I mean, it's like I said: a perfect day. Why ruin it with Shakespeare?*

*The latch clicks on the door to the garage, and my mother slips into the kitchen. She's early. Only halfway through an eighteen-hour shift at the hospital.*

*"Mom. Hi." My hand goes to my hair. It's a mess, of course. I'm not totally awake yet.*

*She doesn't notice. She doesn't even answer me. "Is your father here?"*

*"Work, probably." Weird question. Where else would he be on a Tuesday morning? Or any morning, for that matter.*

*She nods absently, her gaze shifting to the pile of laundry on the floor of the den. Maybe I'll fold it when she leaves again. She'll know it was me; I won't even tell her.*

*She isn't really seeing it, though. Her mind is on something else. She chews her next word around a few times before speaking it. "West?"*

*I raise my eyebrows. What is wrong with her? "School. Can we have pizza for dinner? Just this once?"*

*She focuses on me then, as though noticing me for the first time. "Where is West, Charlotte?"*

*"Mom. It's Tuesday. He's at school. I just said." Like he'd ever miss during the week before exams. I, on the other hand, am not allowed back in classes until fall, if then, so my days will consist of waiting for West to take a break in his never-ending cycle of studies and tests, punctuated by the occasional competition in nerdery or pre-OPT training session.*

*It goes without saying that I am not exactly allowed around any of my old friends these days. A rule I'm happy to keep, for once. Kip and Kingston know I want out. We played a dangerous game, and now that the meteor is coming, the stakes are even higher.*

*So every time Kip calls my cell, I hit ignore, and every time I hit ignore, I become a little stronger. A little more hopeful. And he calls less and less. Sometime soon, he'll stop calling altogether.*

*Heck, maybe if I stay away long enough, they'll all forget I ever existed. Cassa probably already has. I could make a clean break. Finish school. Maybe even train for a specialized job on an Ark and get extra points in the lottery. And once I make it onto an Ark, who knows what's possible? Rumor has it they'd train anyone—anyone—for an advanced degree up there. I could be a nurse, and work for my mom. I rub the arm of the couch, thinking.*

*I could be a doctor.*

*And dolphins could start flying, too, as long as we're making up fairy tales. I close my eyes. Right now, right in this moment, even fairy tales are not out of reach.*

*The door to the garage slams, louder than necessary, and we both jump. I turn to exchange a look with my mother, but she is frowning toward the source of the noise.*

*"Where is she? Where is she." My father's voice fills the room before his presence, an impressive feat on its own. Coupled with his stature, which tends to make grown men shift their shoulders around when they talk to him, it's not hard to see why he's never lost an election.*

*"In here, Michael," Mom calls, her voice barely carrying.*

*"Same place as when you left this morning," I say cheerfully.*

*My father squares up to the kitchen island. "Well?" he says, his pitch rising.*

*I look at him. "Hel-lo? I'm right here, Dad."*

*"What do you know about this?" He slaps a plastic bag onto the counter. The lid on the coffee canister rattles nearby—a little silver fox atop a snowy crystal mountain. Why my parents don't keep their coffee grounds in the same plastic container they bought them in is beyond me. Other than appearances, of course.*

*I turn my attention to the bag and recognize its contents right away. It's twitch, a chemically modified form of valium. People call it that because you twitch when you take it too often. Just one of many, many reasons I've never tried it. This particular sample is in little packets, not pressed back into pills, so it's probably laced with a nicotine synth for an extra kick on the front end and the added benefit—to the dealer—of making you miss it even more when it's over. Probably popular with school kids working their way toward the hard stuff.*

*When it comes to drugs, I don't touch 'em. I like to be in control. I like to think clearly, especially on a job, and I like to win, which is significantly more difficult when, say, you're trying to crack a safe, but your hands are twitching.*

*Just for example.*

*Besides, Kingston didn't like us getting jacked up. He'd call interference. As in, someone had interfered with his income.*

*As in, you do not want to be that person. Trust me.*

*Kip was never one to learn from his mistakes, with one exception: the day we showed up to case some fancy prep school dorm, and he couldn't keep his eyes on the first lock on the gate. It was a basic one, as I recall. Aluminum at most, with a magnetized inner mech. Two polarized pins and you're done in under a minute, easy. Kip fumbled for about ten seconds before Kingston grabbed his jaw in his hand, palm flat, looked into his eyes, and scoffed. Then he sent us straight home.*

*Well. He sent me home. I have no idea where he sent Kip, but I didn't hear from him all night, and I never saw him high again. I had shivered on the walk home, even though it was August, and my back was dripping sweat underneath my pack. For the first time, I had wondered what it would take to get free of Kingston forever. Free of all of them. Even Kip.*

*Anyway. No drugs for me. But no matter how many times I tell people that, they don't believe me. I'm a criminal, right? So I must be getting my kicks from somewhere.*

*If they only knew the feeling of beating a safe people twice my age hadn't been able to break, or the way the adrenaline turns to lead in my veins during a job, steadying my hands and evening out my breath, or the way it feels to slip into a shadow without the slightest whisper of noise, inches from a guard, inches from the camera's line of sight, inches from escape, then believe me, they'd stop asking me how I got my kicks.*

*"Well?" The full circle of flesh underneath my father's jaw took on a tinge of red, snapping me back to the present. He'd gained weight during my last turn inside. "What do you have to say about that?"*

*"Uh, nothing?" I shrugged. "I've never seen it before. I don't even know what it is."*

*"I can tell when you're lying, Charlotte."*

*"Good!" I say, angry. "Then you can tell it's not mine. I have no idea what you're on right now, but I haven't left this house since I got out. And I've never seen those before."*

*My mother presses her tongue into her teeth and looks*

*from me to the marbling on the counter. There's something else on her mind. Something heavier. "Go upstairs, Charlotte," she says quietly.*

*"I'm not done with her," my father says.*

*I roll my eyes and head toward the stairs.*

*He grabs my arm. "You tell me where he got that."*

*I look at him. He isn't nearly as scary as everyone else seems to think. Not to me, anyway. Not compared to Kingston. Besides, what could he possibly do to me that he hadn't already tried? "Who?" I say evenly.*

*"You know who. West."*

*I blink. West?*

*"Start talking, Charlotte. I know you had something to do with this."*

*"Dad. That can't be West's. He doesn't get—he doesn't do stuff like that."*

*"So you do know what it is."*

*I stare at him. "I know it's drugs, if that's what you're asking. Doesn't take a detective."*

*"And?"*

*"And I've never seen it before. Really."*

*He doesn't let go of my arm, and we stare at each other for another moment.*

*"Dad—" I begin.*

*"Get out of my sight. Get out—" he breathes harder, squeezing my arm, trying—and failing—to gain control of either one of us. I keep right on staring. Like I say, he doesn't scare me. "Get out of my house." He shoves my arm when he releases it, throwing me slightly off-balance. I stumble, halfway to the door before I have a second thought.*

*When I look back, the lines around his eyes have changed*

*shape faintly. It's subtle enough that I could have imagined it, but right then, it hits me that it wasn't really anger that made him loud. Fear, maybe. Lack of control, certainly.*

*"Michael," my mom whispers. But she is tired, and worried, and her mind is on West.*

*My father doesn't speak again, so I let the door slam extra hard on my way out.*

*The sun hits me along with the cold air, and I take a deep breath to stretch my lungs. Then I start jogging. I've left my coat, but there's no going back now. It's not too bad out. I can keep moving until I come up with a plan.*

*But the first few blocks roll by, and I have nothing. It's almost ten in the morning, and the cold begins to hurt my face. I still have a few more blocks to go before my nose gets numb. It's too cold to stay outside. I'm getting hungry, and of course I have no money for food. I'll die before I go back to my parents. They don't want me there, anyway. They've gotten used to me being gone. Probably hadn't taken long.*

*I sigh and pick up the pace. Kingston will be awake in a couple of hours. He'll know where Kip is, too. I can keep warm enough until then.*

"Adam! No!" my father was shouting.

The ground fumbled past underneath my feet. I couldn't breathe. There was a sharp ache in my arm, and on investigation, I found that my dad was squeezing it. I struggled, trying to escape the pain, but my vision was obscured by my skin helmet. Which was not ideal, I decided. My helmet should be covering the hole in the ground.

Wait, no. Dad wasn't squeezing my arm. He had an arm around both my shoulders and was gripping me hard enough to break them. I couldn't see much, but his other hand popped the switch in my helmet, releasing oxygen, and I began to gasp. Pain. Pain was everywhere, and we were running.

No, no. Wrong again. Dad was running. I was being carried.

When at last he laid me down, I had a view of the entire hangar. A blue sheet of fire had pasted itself over the white ceiling, its tendrils reaching for both of us. Dad slammed the inner door to the airlock shut, rendering us barely out of its reach, and pulled my helmet off. He stuffed it into the pocket of his skin, and I realized it was *his* helmet, not mine. Adam had pulled mine away to unseal the vacuum.

I touched my head, and my glove came away bloody. My dad pressed my shoulders into his chest, oblivious to the pain that surrounded me.

"Dad! He's getting away!" I shouted, but it came out soft.

Dad cast an anxious glance at Adam's retreating form. "Don't worry about him. Stay with me, Charlotte. *Breathe.*"

I wanted to stand. I wanted to help. I wanted to catch Adam.

I wanted to kill him.

But the fire grew too bright, and my eyes closed against the flames.

# Nine

Somewhere far away, my father was screaming my name. There was an immense crashing sound that repeated itself at intervals, and I began to wince in sync with its intrusive tone. I could not move, but I could hear, and I could feel.

And all I felt was pain. My arm, my face. The side of my head.

My body was on fire.

And someone was hitting me. Hard.

I opened my eyes.

Dad was there, eyes wild, patting out the flames that had ruined my space skin. Bright steel slashed through the air in his fist, turning the skin into ribbons. Now why would he do that?

I breathed in, and my lungs lit up like matches even as the hangar grew dim around me. Everything was fire. Everything was pain.

And then everything was dark again.

*Daddy is taking us camping! He put Mommy and West in charge of the tent, so it's just the two of us now, just me and Daddy, and the woods are green and brown and full of magic. I stomp proudly through the pine needles by his side. We are going to build the fire, the most important part. My arms are full of the kindling I've painstakingly selected: not too thick, not too wet. It's a very grown-up job, and I am determined to behave accordingly. My father's approval shines down from the greenest leaves above us.*

*"Now, Charlotte," Daddy says, not breaking his stride. I hurry my steps to match him, looking up to be sure he sees me. He is as tall as the trees around us. "Three things a fire needs to thrive. Oxygen, heat, and—"*

"EREN!" I screamed, and coughed. "Er—" I forced myself upright on my bad arm, barely able to straighten my head. "Dad!"

But my father was gone, and so was the pain. Half my space skin covered my bad arm, and the other half lay in charred shreds where my father had knifed it off me. I wasn't on fire after all; it was only the suit, and now I was on the other side of the airlock.

I flipped to my belly, intending to stand, and willed my brain to locate Eren while my legs got their bearings.

By the time I was steady, I found him.

He was upside-down, a faceless, bandaged doll in my father's arms, and coming right at me.

He was also on the other side of the lock.

Fear made me stupid, and I struggled to understand what my subconscious was screaming. They were on the other side. They couldn't get here. I breathed fast, too fast, trying to compensate for their declining supply of oxygen. Eren was still unconscious. Dad locked eyes with me, and his panic was infectious.

I scrambled for the lock, yanking it with my left hand

and bracing the turn against my right shoulder. It budged, but only barely.

"Locked. It's locked," I said, like an idiot.

My breath came faster.

Adam couldn't have locked it. Not this soon. As far as I knew, he hadn't even made it through yet.

My breath froze at the thought. If Adam hadn't made it through, then he was almost certainly dead. And if he had died, so had...

*Focus, Char.* Eren's life was still at stake. And my father's.

*Okay. This is a lock. It's a lock. You can do this.*

*You have to.*

There was no way Adam had done this already, so the door had probably sealed automatically when the airlock was compromised. I had to find out what kind of lock I was dealing with, and fast.

*Think, Char. Think.*

My breath came in shaky bursts. I had no information. None at all.

But my dad did.

"Dad!" I shouted through the door. "You have to tell me what sound it made when you opened it!"

"What sound *what* made?"

"The door! The manual release is disabled. I need to know what kind of lock it is! What sound did it make?"

He looked at me. "None!" he said, shaking his head. "I didn't hear anything."

"What about when it closed? Like a pop? Or a metallic sound?"

He shook his head again, and I saw that he'd put the helmet over Eren. "Charlotte, there was a lot going on! I didn't hear it."

73

When you're breaking into a house, it's a good idea to think about *why* its security exists. For instance, you'd be thinking about how to keep out people like me. This puts you in the mindset of the security engineer. From there, you learn everything you can about the system to try to stay a few steps ahead.

I thought about the engineers of the ship. What kind of lock would they use? They weren't trying to keep people out. They were trying to protect against the vacuum of space. I bit a lip, willing my heart to keep beating.

"Magnet," I said. "Gotta be a magnet slider. Set to a computer that can turn it on and off. A door this size, you'd have heard the hydraulics otherwise. Can't be a deadbolt."

Dad stared at me. "Okay. A magnet. How do we fix that?"

"How's my helmet holding up?"

He looked back. "It's there. It's stopping most of the air from escaping, but it's not a perfect seal. I assume that's why life support is off over here. They wouldn't pump oxygen into an airlock once it's depressurized."

"Right. Right." The thought of my father and Eren slowly suffocating threatened to turn my brain into oatmeal. I couldn't think about that right now. I had to fix the magnet. "Heat! Heat can demagnetize the door."

"Yeah. It can also kill us all," Dad said, more quietly this time. "I'm sure they fireproofed it, Charlotte. It's a spaceship."

My hand went to my sleeves. What did I have? What could I use? I had taken scissors and needles from Eren's room, but I couldn't find them now. What did I remember about magnet locks? "If we could get to the magnet, we could redirect the flux lines into a loop. That would kill its field strength."

"I have your scissors on this side," he said, following my thoughts, and I saw that the edges of his mouth were turning slightly blue. "I found them when your space skin was burning. Can you hack the computer? Disable it that way?"

"Hack? No, Dad. I'm not great with computers." There hadn't been a lot of those in juvy.

Locks, on the other hand... those, we had. "Iron," I said. "We need iron. Like a nail, but bigger. If we lay it over the poles, connect them, that'll loop it."

"What?" he shouted, but I was already halfway across the receiving room. There were no panels, no supplies. Just a couple of metal chairs, a table, and some LED-looking lights. It was hopeless.

"Iron!" I screamed. "Iron!" I picked up the chair and flung it into the door, then grabbed a table, aiming its corner at the window. But I was weak, and I only had one hand, and my aim was off. I picked it up and kept right on going anyway.

"Stop! Charlotte! You can't break the window. *It's a spaceship*. It's made of quartz and polyethylene."

Still, I kept hitting it, again and again. Nothing happened. I pressed down against the panic, but knew I was losing. "We—need—iron!"

I was about to watch my father die.

"The nav system in the hopper," he said. "The needle is iron."

I made myself see him, understand his words, but all I wanted to do was scream. Something about his voice calmed me down. "Dad. That's computerized."

"It's *mostly* computerized. People still use compasses in the middle of the route. The polarity orients to the nearest, biggest ship."

"Go get it! Go! And find something you can use to break the—"

But Dad was already halfway back to the hopper. He pulled a flight kit from behind the passenger seat, and I couldn't see what happened next.

I pressed my face into the window, struggling to see Eren, to try to discern whether he was breathing, but he was flat on the ground, and too close to the door, so I couldn't.

Instead, I focused on breathing, and tried to make myself calm. Patient.

I gave up a second later and slapped the window in frustration.

Dad returned approximately one million years after that. He had an ax, a pair of scissors...

And the needle from the compass.

"Okay. What am I doing here?" he said.

*Breathe, Charlotte. Think.* "Hit it with the ax. You gotta dismantle the outer part of the door. It's just cosmetic. Find the magnet."

My dad picked up the ax. He was as tall as the trees.

"Hit it at an angle. You can't break the lock or the actual door. But maybe you can get the outer panel off."

A few whacks later, he looked up at me, then switched to scissors. A second after that, a black panel came away in his hands. He threw it behind himself and rubbed a cheek. His lips were almost totally blue.

"It's gonna look like a deadbolt, Dad. Lay the iron over the poles. Get some surgical tape from Eren to secure it with. Hopefully that will redirect the flux enough that we can muscle the door open. The poles will be positioned near the computer's access—you know what? Just try everything. Every position, once you find the magnet."

"Believe it or not, Charlotte, I've actually seen a magnet before." In spite of everything, Dad smiled. Even his gums were turning blue. "You know, Charlotte—"

"Oh, no. No you don't. Magnet. Poles."

"I'm proud of you. I am, Charlotte."

"*Poles*. Focus. Please, Dad."

A minute later, he nodded at me. "That's... that's either it, or it's as close as I'm going to get. Time to pull."

I braced myself against the frame, locking my wrist against the elbow of my bad arm. I'd wedged some of the space skin into the handle to give myself a better grip, so I pressed my fingers as far into the rubbery fabric as I could. "Okay, *go*."

I pulled for all I was worth.

Inches away, my father did the same.

Nothing happened.

"Come on, *come on*," I muttered through my teeth. We didn't have to pry it all the way open. We just had to open it far enough to disengage the magnet. Maybe only a few inches.

Maybe only one inch.

The door moved. Only a fraction, but it moved. Every millimeter away would weaken the magnet's influence.

I pulled harder.

The door opened an inch, then another inch, and then my father was through, and he was pulling Eren in, but the door wanted to close. I kicked at it, desperate to get Eren through, but my father halted his struggle long enough to block my foot. There was little enough air in the anteroom, but he managed to shout, blue-lipped and wide-eyed, "Don't break it!"

They rolled past me, and my father grabbed the door immediately. We pulled, both of us breathless by this point.

"The other side is magnetized!" I said, but the room lacked the oxygen to carry the sound. I grabbed the ax, planning to reverse my father's work, and life support shut down around us. Too late, I realized that *this* room was now depressurized. We'd all be sealed off together.

To my surprise, the door slid closed on its own a moment later, and I realized that a high-pitched alarm had been reverberating throughout the hangar while it was open. When the door was sealed, it ceased.

My father met my gaze, wild-eyed. We'd done it.

That was when I noticed the soldiers.

They pressed in at the door to the anteroom, hitting it. I saw one helmet, then two. Good. Their door would be released as soon as the anteroom repressurized, then they could help us.

But time ran short on this side of the door. I yanked the helmet off Eren and thrust it into my father's hands. His fingers were a dull blue underneath the nails.

"Oxygen. Quick," I said, and reached for Eren.

Before I could grab him, the hangar ignited once again. I watched, helpless, as the hopper was encased by an explosion a thousand feet wide. I barely caught sight of a tuft of brown hair in the cockpit before the blast obscured my view. The fire was impossibly bright, too bright to look at, and my eyes squeezed shut against the heat.

It took a minute for my heart rate to slow, and once it did, my hand was in full-on shake mode. I peeled the first layer of tape off Eren's eyes, all the way down to the skin, then stopped. Breathed. Checked that Eren was breathing.

Beside me, Dad watched, brows drawn. "He's fine. He'll be okay." His voice was shaky.

I nodded dimly, wondering whom Dad was trying to convince.

Next, I pulled everything away from his ears. Then I turned to the tape on his head. Since he wasn't conscious, I decided to peel it slowly, in the hopes that it wouldn't leave as much of a mark.

Finally, I delicately lifted the tape from his eyelids.

Nothing happened.

"Dad," I whispered, but he didn't answer right away. He was staring at Eren's face.

He'd had an oxygen mask on since before the hull breach, so he'd be fine, right?

"I don't know. I'm feeling kind of..." Dad trailed off, and I looked at him, confused. "Anyway. We need to find the medics. They can help him. Oh, Char. The Ark."

I looked at my dad. "Adam isn't dead. The Ark is fine. Well. As fine as it was when he left it."

He had an expression that made it clear he didn't agree, but his distress was lined with pity. For me.

"Trust me," I said grimly. "He wouldn't go out like that. In fact, he may have had the whole thing planned from—"

"*Stay where you are.*"

Dad jerked his head up, bemused. I looked around, trying to find the source. The metallic voice had a British accent, but the tone was all too familiar.

The door sucked open, abruptly balancing the oxygen, and the voice spoke again.

"Do not attempt to stand."

Slowly, gently, I laid Eren's head on the ground and lifted my arms above my head.

"Ah, good. They're here," Dad said. "We need help," he called. "This young man—"

"No, Dad," I muttered. "Don't."

He looked at me, taking in my posture.

On the other side of the chair, a panel slid open, and a masked team in standard-looking black uniforms poured into the room. They moved quickly, hitting a hasty formation, then readjusting as more and more soldiers rushed in. They were armed, of course. Their ship had just been violently attacked.

But their weapons were aimed at us.

Dad's face went blank, and his eyes locked on mine as understanding set in.

"They're not here to help us," I said quietly. I'd only ever heard that tone in one context. I took a breath and shifted to my knees, keeping my hands up. "They're here to arrest us."

# Ten

Four paces across, four paces back. Square cells were the worst.

They came for me four days later, judging by the strict regimen of lights going on and off, and I can't say I was entirely dreading the moment, at least at first.

I was escorted from my plain white cell in solitary to a plain white room in another part of the ship. On one end of the room, a long, thin table hosted a line of white metal chairs. The final chair stood in the center of the room, alone.

*Oh, goody,* I thought. Another day, another panel of people who controlled my future. Who had already decided what kind of girl I was. Should be fun.

But this was different from a parole hearing or a jury. First off, the guards barely touched me. That was new. Everything felt cordial, civilized. I seated myself in the center chair without prompting. Didn't take a genius to know I wasn't getting a spot at the table.

I shifted a few times, trying to get comfortable, and the skin on my arm prickled, making me think. The lock on the door had taken two men to open. There were no chains on the chair. There were no guards in the room, and the

81

ones who'd brought me here had worn their firearms openly. Whoever else was coming, they must be important. I forced myself to stop fidgeting, aware that I was being watched, then wondered why I cared what they saw.

About the time I stopped moving, six people—three men, three women—dressed in somber suits filed into the room like soldiers and took their seats in unison. None had a gun. They didn't speak at first. They simply regarded me with open expressions. I squeezed my hands together, and six pairs of eyes noticed the tension with half-glances at my lap. That's when I realized that I wasn't just anxious.

I was terrified.

I cleared my throat. "I didn't—"

"I am the captain of this ship, and among us are the ministers in charge of the cities," the man at the center of the table said abruptly. "We are investigating the destruction of a significant portion of our Ark, which took place at the time of your arrival."

I let a breath out slowly. It didn't seem like an invitation to introduce myself.

"We've requested an interview because we find ourselves in the strange position of not having decided what to do with you yet. We have not been able to reach an accord." The captain glanced pointedly at the first place at the table, and I blinked in surprise.

"Charles," I said. My voice carried in the room, and I cringed a little. "Mr. Eiffel."

He gave me a cordial nod, and I searched his eyes for some clue as to my fate. I saw no malice and only the faintest vestiges of our short friendship. For him, five years had passed. In fact, he was basically a blank slate. He probably saw me as nothing more than a dim memory.

"We know each other," I explained shakily. "He was—"

"Mr. Eiffel has given a full statement as to his knowledge of you and your actions. We are far more interested in hearing what you may have to add."

"Let me save you some time," I said. "I don't know how Adam had a bomb, or how he escaped. All I know is that he's probably not dead. He's dangerous and he has a history of working with An, when they find each other useful. And he won't stop until he's back in control."

Another suit let out a beleaguered sigh. "You are not, I think, a killer, Charlotte Turner," she said. She had blue eyes so light they were almost gray, which matched the color of her hair. Her face was pale, and her suit was almost black. In fact, her only coloring came from a shock of coral-red lipstick on her thin mouth. "Your brief tenure as an Ambassador, together with your decisions on board the North American Ark during the attack from the Asian Ark have convinced us that you may yet have something to offer. Assuming, of course, that Adam didn't turn you."

My fear bubbled up into anger. "He hasn't," I said flatly.

"It wouldn't be your fault. Those drugs are powerful. Conceivably, he could corrupt the mind at its very core. Make you think you've seen things you haven't. Make you believe things that are impossible. We've been working on some similar formulas of our own…" She peered at me over the table, letting the threat hang unspoken between us. "Only as a necessary means to developing a counteragent. All we're asking is that you keep your mind open to the idea."

I gave her an irritated glare but held my tongue. Barely.

A fourth suit picked up a stem and adjusted his screen. "Perhaps you'd like to make a statement?"

I wet my lips. "About?"

"Your time as his Lieutenant. Things you may have seen or heard."

I shook my head. "You're right. I was drugged. You can't be sure when it's going on, but coming in and out of it, I knew I was being drugged. I tried to think of ways to escape. It took five years to build up the, the…" I trailed off. "The focus."

The woman with the lipstick peered down her nose at me. "There may be some memories to which you do not have access."

I looked at her. "Then you must believe that I'm innocent. I mean, if I can't even *remember* what he did—"

"As it happens," said the woman, "we do believe in your innocence, Miss Turner. But it does not then follow that you are of no use to us."

The committee looked at each other, and the captain spoke again. "We are going to hold you a bit longer. See what we can come up with. As we said, we have not exhausted our resources yet."

The words made me cold. I drew my shoulder blades together in an effort not to shiver. I needed to think. What was the play here? And what were they planning?

I pressed my lips together. Did I even have a play?

The captain tapped on the table, then stood. Two doors opened at once: his exit, and the one with all the guards, three of whom entered the room and waited for me to stand.

I took in their guns. I wasn't as fast as I used to be, but I could probably make it out the other door before they caught me. I felt a wave of despair. I wouldn't make it far. And then what? I had nowhere to go, except prison. Or execution. The thoughts were equally wearying. The Council members were leaving.

I had nothing to lose, did I? I decided to play the only card I could: the truth.

"Ark Five."

Six suits and three guards froze.

"I might know a little more than I've been letting on."

The captain removed his glasses, wiped them on his tie, then slid them back onto his nose, all while looking directly at me. He sat, and the others followed suit. The lipstick lady nodded at the guards, and they closed the doors, remaining in the room, motionless.

"Very well, Miss Turner. You certainly have our attention."

# Eleven

I waited until everyone had settled back in. "First, I want to know what's happened to Eren and my father."

"I'm afraid that's not possible," said the captain.

"Then I'm afraid I don't know anything about Five."

He gave a sigh. "Miss Turner. We are not your enemies. In spite of what you may believe, we are trying to help."

"I am just about sick of hearing that I'm being locked up for the greater good. Tell me what's happened to Eren. Is he—did he survive?"

The captain took a moment to weigh out his options before deciding to placate me. "Commander Everest is alive. He's in our custody."

"I want to see him."

"I'm afraid that's not possible." He drew a breath, loading it up with whatever threats he planned to level at me, when the lady with the lipstick laid a hand on his arm. "You may not be aware," she said, "but the Arks are designed to need each other."

"So everyone keeps telling me."

"It is more serious than that," she said, glancing at her colleagues for tacit permission before continuing. "We are unable to make planetfall without the assistance of Ark Five."

I looked at her. "Why not?"

"In spite of our most advanced shelter modules, the radiation from the sun would kill us off in less than a generation. Possibly sooner. We needed Ark Five to produce the electromagnetic fields necessary to shield us."

"We need EM poles," the captain explained, "or we cannot produce an atmosphere. We really are quite trapped out here. To find the persons responsible for its destruction..." he touched the table eagerly. Something about their tone inclined me to be more helpful than I usually was with panels and threats and people wearing suits. And adults in general, actually.

All right, fine. Authority in general.

"Okay," I began, "awhile ago, I was in Comm Con in the North American Ark."

"When did you say?" he interrupted.

"I don't know, like a few weeks after the meteor. *Anyway*," I said, "I ended up spending some time on the Guardian Level. I saw the comms. The communications. All of them."

They leaned in, and I found myself mirroring their posture. "I saw one going to Ark Five."

Six pairs of eyes gave me the most skeptical blinks I'd ever seen.

"I know it sounds crazy, but I don't think the Ark was destroyed. I think it's still out there."

"I am sorry to tell you, Miss Turner, but such a thing is not possible," the captain said gravely. "Our scanners have never ceased to search for it."

"Well, you might want to check on those."

Lipstick studied me, rubbing her cheek thoughtfully. "What did it say?"

"It said, *The bird will fly on X.*"

"And whence came this mysterious message?" said the captain. "Did you happen to see that, too?"

I nodded. "Yeah. It came from you."

In the silence that followed, Charles adjusted his jacket, angry. Lipstick pursed her wide mouth into a prim frown. The captain tossed his stem onto the table in frustration, and the others gave an audible groan.

"It did," I said, my voice stronger. "From this Ark. I think it meant the Treaty. I think it was an offer of protection."

The captain sat back in his chair. "Setting aside the fact that I would certainly be aware of any official contact between my Ark and that one, and the sheer imagination required to produce such an idea, let us examine this further. Was the message encrypted?"

"No," I said quietly. "But it was in Morse code. And I never said it was official."

"Morse code," he said slowly. "And you are familiar with that?"

I felt my lower lip push out a little. "No. But I showed it to... a friend. And he told me what it meant." I didn't want to involve Eren any more than necessary until I could be sure he was safe.

"Was the message transmitted in English?" asked the captain.

I closed my eyes. "No. But he—my friend speaks French."

Lipstick rolled her eyes. "And it went directly to Ark Five?"

I forced myself to breath normally. "Well," I said, then

needed to clear my throat. "It went to an Ark, and it wasn't one of the other four. Those were marked. Then there was a big, blank space—"

At this, a second woman who'd been silent up to then picked up her screen and prepared to leave. "This is ridiculous," she said.

I clamped down on my voice, unwilling to let it rise. In my experience, no one listens to girls when they're shouting. "Look. There was a transmission between this Ark and what could only have been another Ark. I'm sure of it."

"A message cannot be transmitted between two Arks by any means but official channels," said Lipstick, her voice equally low. "They receive special designation in every comm system out there. And no one outside of this room has the power to do that from our Ark."

I gave her a dark look. "Then it came from someone in this room." There was a heavy pull on my arm, and I felt myself being lifted to my feet. I gave an angry shrug against the guard responsible, but he had me halfway to the door before I could collect my thoughts.

"Set up a transmitter! Send another message!" I shouted. "I know what I saw. Ark Five is out there. Hey!" I said, jerking against the guard. His grip began to hurt. "It might not be too late to find them!"

The door closed behind me, and I had one final glance at the room. Everyone was preparing to leave, shaking their heads in frustration and even bland amusement. No one so much as watched me go.

Well. No one except Charles.

Ten paces left. Five steps back. Ten paces right. Five more forward.

Repeat.

As cells go, my new digs were bigger than some, not as big as most. The only feature of interest, other than the former senator experiencing his first turn inside, was the enormous mirror in the door.

Well, it was a mirror to me. From the other direction, it—

"Charlotte. You must. *Stop*. Pacing."

"Sorry. I like to get a feel for the space before I settle in. Helps me think."

Dad was seated on the lone mattress, head in hands, facing directly down. He rubbed his hair with both palms, back and forth, back and forth. Everyone's got their tics, even on lockup.

Especially on lockup.

And there was only one reason why they'd keep me in a cell with my father. "So, you know we're being recorded," I said casually. Translation: Don't mention West. "You know that's a two-way mirror."

"Yes, Charlotte. I'm not as dim as I must appear."

"I don't think you're—all right. Sorry."

"We should compare notes," he said.

"Okay," I nodded. "What did they ask you?"

"Oh, you know. How long had I been planning the violent overthrow of the European Ark. Where was the rendezvous with Adam. The usual." His voice had a husky tone, and I wondered whether they'd hurt him. At the same time, I didn't want to know the answer. "What happened to Five. Got that one a few times."

This time, I could hear it in his tone. They had hurt him.

He lifted his head, and I wondered if one side of his face looked swollen, or if I were imagining it. "You?"

90

I shrugged. "Not much, actually. They took my blood a few times. Asked about Adam. I had a fun meeting with a bunch of suits in a big white room. They wanted to know if I was under any foreign influences. You'd have liked them."

"What'd you tell them?"

"You mean, other than the ones that put the handcuffs on?"

He sighed, unamused.

"I told them he's dangerous," I said. "My other meetings were a lot more colorful. No suits, for one. No exposed faces, either."

He raised an eyebrow.

"I gave them everything they asked for. I even drew maps of the control room."

"Charlotte, they're probably planning—"

"A takeover? Maybe." I shrugged. "But anything is better than what it's been for the past five years."

He gave a short, resigned nod. "Do you get the sense that they feel sympathetic toward the people on the Ark, at least?"

"Are you asking if they're going to blow it up, like An was planning? I don't think we can put it past anyone anymore. I mean, they asked you about Five, right? Clearly, it's on the table. Did they mention Eren?"

"No," he said briefly. His face was pale; his tone, distracted. Something else was going on in his head.

"Well, did you ask about him?"

"No. I was... preoccupied by other lines of thought."

"Have they found Adam?" I asked.

"Of course not. They say he never got on the Ark. He was on the hopper when it blew."

I snorted. "Sure. They didn't see it, so it must not have happened. Dad, they never found the pieces of the hopper."

"There wouldn't have been much to find, based on what I saw. They may be right, Charlotte." He rubbed his knuckles twice, then went back to his scalp.

"Then he died in space. Along with our entire Ark. And we'd know about it."

"It's fairly typical to withhold information during an interrogation," he said quietly.

"The destruction of an entire Ark is hardly routine information, Dad."

He stopped rubbing his scalp. "Speaking of—they did mention the sphere a few times. On this Ark." His tone was soft and slow. Hesitant. Like he was trying to decide whether to keep talking.

I looked up. "What sphere?"

"The city-sphere closest to the landing pad. It was completely destroyed."

I felt cold. "*City?*"

Dad nodded. "Whole thing took a hit, apparently."

"Oh." That was—I tried to picture it, but I just couldn't. All those people. "Oh, Dad."

"If he is alive, then we have to find him, Charlotte."

I looked at him. His face was different from mine. On second glance, I saw that it wasn't swollen at all. It was pulled tight, with tinges of red.

Dad wasn't horrified. He wasn't in shock, or pain. At least not physically.

He was furious.

It was several more seconds before I caught up to him. And when I did, it was like falling off a frozen cliff and down into a vast, barren ocean.

"West," I breathed. "Mar—"

"That's enough," he said, and I shut up. This was not the time to advertise the names of our family members.

"We have to find him," I agreed, and he nodded. But neither one of us was talking about my brother. "We have to kill him."

The days passed, and we were presented neither the opportunity to escape nor the chance to assassinate our former tyrant. Aloud, we wondered whether Adam had regained control of the North American Ark or just disappeared. Both things we had already mentioned to our interrogators. We couldn't talk about anything to do with our family, so once our scant speculation had ended, we simply stayed quiet.

While we were made wary by the surveillance, we were just as careful about each other. And it wasn't long before the silence grew thick and strong in the tiny cell we shared with it, fed by memories of the pain we'd volleyed back and forth since I was young. A day passed without conversation, and then two, and I did not know if the quiet served to shelter us from our guilt or strangle us by it. But I came to dream of the day we could escape and leave those conversations on the floor of the cell, unspoken.

I longed to fight, to kill, to win back my brother and my ship.

I did not long to remember. I did not long to forgive. My father must have felt the same, I decided, since he didn't speak either.

So I slept, and my father crowded my dreams. I woke, and there he sat, silent, tallying up the sins of his daughter and worrying over the life of his son. His face grew thin,

93

and he stopped eating. Dark circles bloomed underneath his eyes, resting just above his sunken cheeks. He rubbed his head constantly. A low, persistent level of fear ran through me as I wondered over the fate of my family and my ship. Isaiah and Eren. I shoved everything out of mind. I slept as much as I could. I thought wistfully about being in stasis, when I didn't have to think at all. I shut that thought out, too.

I worried I was going crazy. I worried that it didn't matter if I did.

The light in the cell never altered, and our food, some kind of unholy vegetable-protein synth, was delivered by hands—or hydraulics—unseen. One day, as I lay on the cot, the room grew suddenly dark. I gasped, and my father stood over me. I couldn't see his face, just the outline of his shoulders, which I traced down, down, until I realized that his arms ended at my neck.

He had always wanted me dead, hadn't he? Not out loud, and probably not even consciously. But deep down, he had to have known that was a better situation than the one I'd put him in: a rich, powerful man who couldn't even control his own daughter. Who had to have special press conferences at every re-election, addressing his child's latest troubles. Who could never run for president, or High Commander.

Who hadn't gotten me out of prison, because when I was inside, he could sleep at night, knowing I was finally contained.

And then he was strangling me. I tried to breathe, but my neck was closed. My head jerked back and forth, to no avail. I screamed, but only a gurgle came out. So I kicked him. One leg, then the other, then both, again and again. His chest was made of rubber, and nothing happened.

I screamed, over and over, until at last the lights returned, and my father's voice filled the cell alongside my own.

"Charlotte? Charlotte. Wake up!"

"NO! Dad, stop!" I twisted back and forth and fell sideways off the flimsy cot. When my legs hit the floor, I came fully awake. But I didn't stop screaming. I couldn't.

I kicked at him, over and over, until I finally landed a blow. He withdrew his hands, which were at my elbow, not my neck, and his shoulder hit the wall. I raised my hands to my neck, protecting it, but its only ache came from inside my throat.

His eyes were narrowed, and his voice was overly calm: the tone people use when they're trying to make *you* calm. When they're trying to control you.

That tone had always made me angry, and today was hardly the exception. I continued to scream, unable to form thoughts or words, and the mirrored panel slid open. Hands grabbed my father, forcing him down onto his knees.

"Wait!" he said, and fear gave his voice an edge. "She needs—"

More hands, this time for me. I kicked them, too, and the crack of a stunner penetrated the wall in my brain.

"Stop!" Dad was screaming. "STOP!" A knee in his chest. A stunner in mine.

It ignited, and the world exploded into electric stars.

One final scream, the last of the oxygen pressed out of my lungs. I struggled to inhale, but I couldn't, and blackness slipped in around the edges of the stars. It was relatively quiet as my arms were bound behind my back, but when they pulled me to my knees, then up to my feet, I could finally breathe again.

The door opened, and coherent thought returned to me.

95

Well. *One* coherent thought returned. I would never be safe. I could never be loved. The only person who cared for me had died in my place, and now I was alone in the universe.

You could trap me in a cell with someone else, and I would always be alone. Case in point.

So I took my breath, and the guards hustled me toward the door.

I looked back at my father. His face was stricken with panic. The lower part of his nose was rimmed in fresh blood. One part of my brain decided that someone must have hit him. He was pleading with the guards, telling them something, but I couldn't hear what.

The doors began to close between us, and we locked eyes. And I realized I'd been screaming my one coherent thought since before the stunner blasted me. And finally, I heard it. It sliced through the silence that had grown hard in our cell, cutting it off cleanly at the root.

*"YOU LEFT ME TO DIE!"* My jaw locked in pain, but the words came out again and again. Everything else was just an act between us. A pantomime. The door to the cell was locked between us, but I screamed at the wall. I screamed at my father. *You left me to die.* Not just at the end of the world, but every night I spent in a cell on Earth before that. Half my childhood, lost to fear and darkness. And my father hadn't bothered to save me.

You left me to die.

You left me to die.

You left me to die.

96

# Twelve

I came to in a hospital bed at the end of a long room full of other beds behind curtains. I jiggled my wrist to confirm it was chained, and then my ankles. Metallic clanks answered.

Authority was so predictable.

Although, they'd known I would try to escape, so maybe I was, too.

I blinked. My eyes hurt. Actually, my everything hurt. My muscles were sore from seizing up at the stunner.

On the bright side, I didn't feel like I was drugged. And on the very bright side, I was no longer in the holding cell.

The last time I'd been in a clean, white bed like this, Isaiah had come to me. So had Eren. I realized that I missed them both. Perhaps it was the change of atmosphere, but my head was clearer, too.

I thought about my dad, and about my screaming. I regretted that. I could have lived the rest of my life without pulling that up from the ground we'd buried it in. We could have gone on being together, being a family, if it weren't for me. The thought was painfully familiar.

I briefly considered whether I'd been drugged, but

dismissed the idea. I probably wasn't. And it didn't matter, anyway. The damage was done. Past. I'd have to live with it now. That thought was familiar, too.

"Ah, ah," came a voice. Its tone carried a light warning.

I twisted my head toward it, and my vision followed a split second later. An orderly was reading my vitals off a screen.

"You cannot escape. We're ready this time."

See? Predictable. I rolled my eyes—a *huge* mistake, it turned out; my brain pulsed in pain—and then stopped. As far as I could remember, I'd never escaped from a hospital before. Or from anywhere on board the EuroArk. How could I? The guards here loved their guns as much as the Commander ever had, and they'd never taken any chances with us on lockup. I couldn't even see the people who'd fed us.

"This time?" I asked innocently. If I could get him talking, maybe I could find out what happened to the North American Ark. And Eren.

But he wandered away, ignoring me.

My next opportunity arrived with the doctor. I heard her voice before I saw her. She was talking to another patient, then an orderly, in a muffled tone before rounding the corner to my bed. She had a tight blonde bun and clear blue eyes. In contrast to the orderlies around her, she wore a tailored white coat over a sea green uniform.

"We have a lot of questions about you," she observed in a flat tone. She sounded Irish, but I wasn't sure. Maybe she'd lost some of her accent during her training. Her voice was naturally soft, but her tone carried enough confidence to give her an easy air of authority. "But none that cannot wait," she finished crisply. "Follow the stem with your eyes." It slid back and forth before me, and I obeyed. "Not quite there yet. I do not approve of their methods," she tutted, "but in your case, perhaps we were justified."

"What methods? Locking us up? Drugs? *Did you drug me?*"

She observed my anger without much of a reaction.

"Look," I said. "I know about the city. I'm sorry. All those people. But we had nothing to do with that. That was—"

"Adam. Yes, we know."

I stared at her. "Then why have I been in a jail cell for the past week?"

Her eyes lingered on my face, then slid to the screen in her arms. "Week?" she said neutrally. The stem scrawled over the screen, out of my view.

"Yeah. I've spent at least a week locked up in your jail, and I didn't do anything wrong."

She pursed her lips, as though she couldn't agree with that assertion, and took a breath. "You've been locked up for months. They're waiting for the story to die down. And to be honest, they don't exactly know what to do with you." Her head cocked to the side, and she continued her exam, shining a light in my eyes, pressing back my fingers. Examining my right arm, running a firm finger over the amputation scar, which had lightened considerably over the last five years. "No fluid retained. Vitals are fine." She plopped the screen down onto the bed next to me and tossed the stem on top of it.

I forced my eyes not to follow it. If I were going to steal it, as I certainly intended to do, I had to help her forget it existed first. "If you're wondering whether I'm working with Adam somehow, let me clear that up right now. Help me find him, and I'll kill him myself."

"On this Ark, you are not necessarily considered a killer, Miss Turner. But he had you under his control for years. He made your mind weak. We can't discount the possibility that he turned you." Her voice was as tight as her bun. I bit a lip and reminded myself that I should probably try to sound as far from crazy as possible.

"I'm not working with Adam," I said. "I tried to bring him to you. He tried to kill me as soon as I got here. He's not dead, either."

"That's not what the deck vids show."

"And you're right. I'm not a killer, either. But in his case, I'd make an exception."

"So what are you, Charlotte Turner? Are you a rebel? A hero?" The words mocked me. She folded her arms, letting the question hang. "Little of both? We've all heard about you disarming your Ark. And the stasis."

"Then you know why I had to leave. Adam is a monster. Worse than a murderer."

"That's as may be. But you brought him to us, Turner. You brought your killer tyrant to our peaceful Ark. And then you set him free."

I gave her a long, considered sigh. "To be fair, I thought you guys could handle him. I mean, he was unconscious, as far as I knew. And unarmed." I paused, letting my voice trail off a little. "And outnumbered... and tied up. And you had your own little army, all set to go as soon as we got here, but hey. My mistake." I broke the gaze to look away, then snapped back. "Wait. How do you know that?"

"How, what now?"

"How do you know any of that?" I demanded.

"We know about the disarmament because there were Tribune officials on every Ark, including the Asian one. And they talked," she said casually. "We know about Adam the same way. We know you brought him here because your arrival was recorded. Everything here is. And we know all of the above because our officials don't *hide information* from us." Her voice slid down a tick on the last bit, as though to point out the differences between her government and mine.

"That you know of," I muttered. She ignored that. "Wait. What do you mean, *were*? There were Tribune officials on every Ark? Where are they now?"

"No one knows. No one cares. The Treaty of Phoenix has been held in abeyance since the city-sphere blew up. It's been on shaky ground since your Ark fell to Adam anyway. He's not exactly the rights-to-the-people champion we'd be comfortable dealing with. The Tribune has no power here. Or anywhere else."

I stared at her, trying to grasp the implications of what she was telling me, all thoughts of the screen stem abandoned. "So, it's every Ark for itself?"

She nodded tersely.

"That's—but that's a disaster. I mean, it's fine for you. For Asia, even. But what about the Arks with no weapons?"

"We are peaceful. And Asia won't attack anyone who's not a threat. So far, the only warmongering Ark out here is yours."

"What happens when we get to Eirenea?"

She took a moment before replying, and then another. Finally, she popped a lock on the bottom of my bed, and I realized that it was on wheels, like a gurney. The bed began to roll toward the door.

"Field trip?" I asked.

In response, she pointedly grabbed the screen—and the

101

stem—off the bed, placing them well out of my reach. I sighed, but it wasn't much of a loss. I had one arm, and it remained handcuffed. My odds of escape weren't exactly high, at this point.

"Seriously, where are you taking me?"

We reached the end of the white room and slid out of the exit, turning sharply to the right. I didn't know enough about the inner layout of this Ark to figure where we were relative to the spikes or the spheres, but a massive hologram came into view at the end of the hall in front of me. The doctor pressed me forward, faster and faster, until we reached the glass, and I gasped. It was breathtaking: an absolutely enormous curved surface, spinning slowly and surrounded by stars. I stared, speechless, and felt my mouth open.

"That's—that's—" I stuttered finally. "It's not a hologram, is it." The deep, reddish-gray surface slid past the porthole, only miles beneath my feet, and I gripped the rail of the gurney without thinking. It was like falling *around* a planet.

Or a planetoid, actually.

"That's Eirenea," the doctor whispered. "We achieved planetary orbit while you were out."

I swallowed, soaking in the sight before me. Humanity's new habitat. Eirenea was our hope for a future, and it was beautiful. Dark, like slate, with shallow craters. A few cracks, where maybe one day, we could build rivers. I'd heard rumors there were scientists who could synthesize water and soil from other compounds, and I gasped at the thought. *We could plant trees. We're going to have lakes again, and roads.*

*We're going home.*

"We did it," I breathed. "We actually made it." I twisted around to look at the doctor. Was it like this every time? Was it as beautiful to her now as it must have been a month ago? Her face was tight, like mine, but her mouth pulled into a bitter frown.

"We've done nothing. One month in, and they can't even decide where to start. No Ark wants to make planetfall. People say it will divide our resources too much, leaving the Arks vulnerable to attack. Even if they did land a ship, we can't terraform without an electromagnetic field."

I looked back to Eirenea, breathing it in. "So let's build one."

"We don't have the power. The Treaty was designed to make us interdependent, to keep us from going to war. Every ship needs something from the other ships. But so far, all it's done is cripple us."

She turned the bed to wheel it away, and I twisted in my sheets, willing us to stay put. "Wait! Don't make me leave. I just want to watch for a little while."

Her face softened, and I thought I saw a twinge of regret. Or sympathy. But the gurney moved quickly back to sick bay. "I have to get back to work," she said. "I'm on duty."

I looked at her. "Please. Let me stay out there. It's not like I can go anywhere." I rattled my cuff at her.

"I'm afraid it's almost time for the shift change," she said, punching the door pad and wheeling us through. "I have to transfer custody. It would not go well for me if I left Charlotte Turner sitting in the hallway."

"No. It wouldn't," said a voice.

I jerked around, facing forward. Bright red hair split the pasty walls and white curtains of the bay, and my face lit up in a smile. Marcela. *Mars*. Alive. And here, in the flesh.

In a tailored white coat, too, and a sea-green uniform under that. "Thank you, doctor. I can take it from here," she said calmly.

103

The two doctors exchanged codes, waiting while their screens shared information, and the blonde doctor nodded and prepared to leave.

"So. Charlotte Turner," said Mars, watching her go. "What *are* we going to do with you?"

# Thirteen

"How are we feeling today?" Her eyes slid down to the screen, then back to mine. Her voice was calm. Clinical. And undeniably Polish.

Okay.

"I can't believe you're here! This is—How did you—"

Her eyebrow raised a tenth of a millimeter—barely at all—and I clamped my mouth shut. Not my smartest moment.

"They did mention you had the brain fried," she said lightly in her new accent, pursing her lips to suppress a smirk. "Sorry for that."

"Sure you are. I'm feeling fine, *doctor*. Thanks for coming to see me." I squeezed my eyes shut, wishing I could make my brain work faster. It was harder than it should have been. Mars was actually a doctor. But she was more of a soldier than a doctor, I reasoned, thanks to her training at the Academy. Either way, she was the kind of girl who knew exactly what she was doing, even when everyone else stayed a step behind.

None of that explained what she was doing in the sick bay right then.

"Don't mention. Really." Her tone was nearly bored, and

like I said, Polish. Just, so Polish. "Dr. Karam may have told you," she said, her accent trilling the words, "but we're anxious to assess the extent of the ongoing influence the drugs have on your mind." A hand slid down the screen, then back up again. Her short nails were as red as her hair. She tapped the stem against the edge of the screen and repeated the whole process. I frowned. Mars wasn't one to fidget. As far as I knew, she rarely wasted a motion.

But then again, she also wasn't Polish, so what did I know?

"You can't seriously think he turned me," I ventured, more careful now.

"As I said. We look forward to making sure. A few more tests, maybe a personality profile. And then we take closer look." Her accent was absolutely grating by now, but I ignored it, picking up a sinister edge in her tone.

"Closer... how, exactly?"

"Oh, do not worry; it doesn't hurt. We shave the back of the head and make small incision, then remove part of skull. You will be awake the whole time! Save you *many* hair-brushing!" she said brightly, then frowned. "Well. It would. If you did that already. We should have everything we need by third or fourth extraction."

"Ex—*what?!* No. No, no, no."

"No?" she said, glancing up from the screen. The stem hit the bed, inches from my hand.

"No."

"Ah. Okay. We move to Plan B, then. Is more my style, anyway."

I wet my lips, and visions of razors and mind control danced through my head. She'd never been particularly fond of me, but I hoped for my brother's sake that her next plan would involve significantly fewer scalpels. Assuming they were still together. I swallowed. Assuming he was still alive, even. "And... what might that be?" I asked timidly.

Her face split into a smile, and I saw that she'd been concealing a laugh for a while now. She turned and slammed a hand into the alarm button on the wall near my bed. "Duck and cover, Turner. Now."

I blinked, and time slowed.

Mars reached across the bed to grab my hand in hers. With her other hand and the rest of her body, she slammed the gurney sideways, flipping it onto its side.

I hit the floor on my hip, less painfully than I'd expected to, and she came flying over the top of the bed.

"That was the duck?" I muttered.

She pulled the mattress over our heads and nodded, finally speaking in her usual voice. "This is the cover. Should have seen your face, though." She laughed. "Classic. Hang in there, Charlotte. You're doing great!"

"Should have heard your accent, though," I muttered. I fiddled with the stem, trying to unlock the cuff around my wrist, and she pulled a face.

"Well," she amended slowly. "You're doing fine, anyway."

The cuff rattled louder, and I fumbled the stem, then tried to catch it with my other hand.

Which had been amputated five years earlier.

The stem hit the linoleum and rolled away, just out of reach. At the same time, my side of the mattress slid down, exposing us.

"Well," she said quietly, as though to herself this time. "You're not dead yet, anyway."

"Ugh, sorry, sorry," I muttered, yanking against the cuff

in frustration. I tried to straighten the mattress with my unchained arm, but lacking a hand on that arm, I couldn't keep it from sliding right back down. Mars watched, a look of silent disbelief on her face. Across the room, obscured from our view by the sideways gurney, the door slid open, and a red light began to flash. I sucked in a breath, frustrated. That had to be a silent alarm, and judging by the number of booted footsteps, we weren't alone in the room any more.

"Be warned. You are under arrest. Release your hostage. Hold your position with your hands in the air." The admonition was punctuated by a smatter of what sounded like rubber bullets against the exposed bottom of the gurney.

Beside me, Mars pulled a mouth filter out of her coat pocket, shaking her head, and placed it between her teeth. Then she bent over her watch as though counting the seconds.

There was a bang, followed by a crack of smoke, and my throat began to close. Mars shoved a second filter into my mouth, and I bit down, sucking in clean air.

When the smoke spread, she threw herself out onto the floor under its cover and grabbed the stem. My handcuff popped open a second later, and she yanked me by the wrist, pulling us to our feet. The smoke doubled in volume, and then doubled again. It was so thick that I couldn't see my hand in front of my face. The bullets stopped, but the footfalls didn't.

We made our way to the side of the room, where the smoke was thinner. Mars pressed me forward, but a soldier appeared to my left. I made to hit him on the jaw, but he was wearing a masked helmet, and I struck plastic, effectively disabling my only hand. Great.

I ducked back into the smoke, dodging his outstretched arm, and grabbed his gun. Old habits, and all that.

He stumbled, and I hit him over the head, intending to knock him out.

Again, I struck plastic. He ducked into the smoke.

"Honestly," said Mars, shaking her head again. She rapped against the wall frantically, then turned back to me. "Aim the gun at *me* this time." She gestured meaningfully to the smoke, where the soldier appeared again.

"Sorry," I grunted, and pointed it at Mars. He froze. It was light in my hands, probably due to the nonmetal bullets, and I smiled. "Turn around and start walking, or I shoot her," I said to him, my words garbled by the filter. I was sounding a lot more upbeat than I meant to. It was good to be armed again. And free, for the moment. The guard complied.

Behind us, a panel slid off the white wall, revealing the outline of a man. Dark glasses. Dark skin.

Mars popped the filter out of her mouth in an irritated jerk to speak to him. "Just—just take her. Please."

Hands, warm and sure, grabbed me around the waist, pulling me close and pressing me through the panel. I breathed in, then pulled out my filter. "Isaiah."

"Hello, little bird."

"*Isaiah.*"

"Yes." His hand found mine. He was dressed as a Guardian. I hadn't known they had those on this Ark.

"Ise—" I began a third time, but he cut me off, smiling.

"We'll catch up later, what say?"

I swallowed and tasted sulfur. He pressed me through the panel and into a crawlspace. From there, we skimmed along a wall and into an adjacent room. An office, from the looks of it. Mars and Isaiah ran for the door, which was on a different wall than the one in the sick bay. I followed as fast as I could. It led to a new, open hallway, free and clear. For now, at least. We broke into a full sprint, Isaiah first, and me trailing several steps behind, winded. To my surprise, Mars was about as slow as I was, and breathing about as hard. When we were halfway down the hall, the flashing red lights broke out again.

We crowded through another door, then another, until I thought my lungs would explode. At last, we folded ourselves into a low supply closet. I'd tried to keep my bearings, but it was nearly impossible. I figured we were maybe halfway out on a spike and headed toward the massive sphere at the center of the Ark.

"This is where we stop. Wait for the signal," Isaiah said to me, then he turned to Mars. "You got me worried back there."

Mars shrugged. "She's really off her game. Nothing like you said."

"*She* is armed now," I said pointedly. "And she can hear you."

"And I'm really scared, let me tell you," said Mars. "Especially after that demonstration of your mythical abilities. That was some of the worst escaping I've ever seen."

"Oh? Well, that was the worst fake accent I have ever heard. No, literally. The worst."

She pressed a patient sigh out of her nose. "I'm afraid I'm just not cut out for the theatre. Anyway, look. I had to be European. Not that you'd appreciate this, but it took some effort to get me in there."

"So why not be, oh, I don't know, *Spanish*? Seems a no-brainer."

"No wonder you thought of it, then. But for your information, I'm Honduran. Different accent. Different *continent*, actually. But that was some awesome work with the stem there, Char. Inspired, really."

I raised my voice, attempting to mimic her Polish accent. "Hey, let us sit around to play the mattress forts while One-Armed Wonder does the magic escape! Is solid plan, am right? Never mind bullets. Are rubber."

"Um, excuse me, but whose rescue op is this, anyway? Still mine? Shut up, then. And here," she said, shoving Isaiah's pack at me. "Get some real clothes on." She glanced at me in the half-light, and I saw that she was smiling. I smiled back, and slid into a dark corner of the closet to change.

It was actually pretty great to see her. Not to mention Isaiah. I wondered what he'd been up to for the past five years, but before I could ask, the red alarm lights were replaced by blue ones. They illuminated the floor at the bottom of the door. "That's the signal," he said, his voice low. "Let's move."

This time, as we sprinted through the cavernous hallways of the EuroArk, we started seeing people. After the third strange glance at a doctor running around with fire-red hair, a Guardian, and their fairly winded sidekick, Mars began to look nervous.

"That's my cue," she whispered. She peeled away from us, and I looked after her, surprised. She caught my expression and laughed. "Good to see you, Char. Really."

Isaiah nodded his goodbye. "See you on the flipside, Mars. Be well."

I stopped my awkward, panting, sprint-walking to watch her go. She faded into a side hall and out of sight. The hallway felt emptier, somehow.

Isaiah took me by the elbow. "Let's keep on it. We still have a ways to go."

"Where *are* we going?" I asked, suddenly worried. "I have questions." More than anything, I wanted to ask about West, and whether they had a plan to rescue my father.

And Eren. I hadn't spotted him during my brief, non-smoky, fully conscious moment in the sick bay.

I was also anxious to hear about Maxx, the lockie from the cargo hold of the North American Ark who'd been friends with Amiel. But I knew better than to mention names, or even refer to other people. I wasn't sure what kind of surveillance this Ark had, but I was willing to bet my left hand that someone would be watching a vid of this moment in the very near future.

"Not to worry," he said gently. "You'll see soon enough."

"So what was that thing you set off back there? You doing bombs now?"

"A microwave, in fact. An 80-watt, circuit-breaking microwave with an antenna, if you want to get technical about it. It's older mech, but it works just fine. Knocks out most of their signals. S'why we aren't being chased. The cameras are running, but the vid feeds are down." He gave me what seemed like a long glance through his glasses and slid through an inner port.

The passageways were much wider here. I figured we were nearing the enormous sphere at the center of the Ark. He stepped quickly, without feeling his way, and I frowned. Something was off. Not with his voice, or his mannerisms. And it wasn't his confidence, either. That was the same Ise I'd always known.

"I'm glad you didn't use a bomb, for what it's worth, Ise," I said, and it hit me. He was *moving* differently, like he knew his way around. But that wasn't possible, was it?

He nodded. "I'm nonviolent now."

112

When it came to Isaiah, I'd always found it wise to hold onto a thin strain of skepticism. Right then, my strain was big enough to fill the entire hallway. "Says the guy who once overthrew an entire Ark."

We stood at the end of the passage, in front of an enormous port. The ship stretched out around us, as wide as I'd seen it. Isaiah put a hand on the door, then slid the circular latch open without effort. A small smile played across his lips, and he chuckled. "Don't be so dramatic, Char. It doesn't suit you."

"I'm not the one who just appeared in a cloud of smoke, Ise."

This time, he laughed out loud, like I was finally catching up to the joke. And maybe I was. "Any other questions?" he asked, teasing. "I know you got 'em."

"Oh, I have so, so many. But if I had to narrow it down, I'd start with this one: Isaiah, can you see?"

# Fourteen

By now, I was smiling, too, but the thought was too strange to swallow. "You can, can't you?" Isaiah had been blind since around the time they announced that no one with a major disability would be allowed on board an Ark. Not by coincidence, of course, but at the hands of his own brother. I supposed that he thought he was protecting the family—their mother especially—from Isaiah, who'd given her more than her share of worry. I pictured his brother's face, guarded and hard, and I had no comfort from the thought of his death in the meteor. "You can see."

He held his hands out, an open gesture of invitation, and the moment was heavier than it should have been. Finally, I reached up to lift his glasses off his face. My hand was steady, to my immense relief, but my heartbeat was not.

Silver eyes gazed back at mine.

"What," I breathed, unable to complete the thought. Isaiah continued to smile, looking at me. His face was serious beneath his grin. A moment later, I smiled, too. "Is that—are they mechanical? Some kind of transplant?"

He paused, still staring, before breaking the moment. "Prosthetic." He took the glasses back and folded them carefully into a pocket. "A whole system, actually. It captures images and converts them into electrical pulses. Built from the same tech they've had on earth for decades. But the implant transmits them to the neural pathways. It's like watching a stop-motion film," he said, looking up to the ceiling, then at the walls, and finally, back at me. "I am told the processors will improve in the coming years, but I don't mind. The effect is somewhat... lovely."

I touched a tiny scar on the side of his eye, just above his cheek. It was jagged and angry. Not the work of a surgeon. "This is from your brother."

Isaiah nodded solemnly. "He loved me once, you know?"

Of course I did. I was suddenly anxious to get to wherever it was we were going, and I pressed into the door, which didn't open. Isaiah put a hand on mine, stopping me, and in response, I pushed harder.

"There are things we can never heal, Char. I've made my peace with that."

*No kidding, Ise.* I took a breath and yanked the door back instead. It flew open. "Good for you. Let's go."

He gave me a look like he'd known I'd react that way. Like my scars were written on my face as plainly as his own. He took the door from me, holding it steady. "After you, little bird."

I'm not sure what I expected the sphere to look like, but it was striking enough that I supposed I hadn't considered it.

An immaculate hall stretched before me, and I knew instinctively that it was perfectly straight. In fact, it was a perfect square. It was vibrantly blue, not as though it had been painted, but as though it would still be blue if you took a knife to the wall and dug a scratch in it.

Not that anyone had scratched anything in here. It was pristine. Untouched.

A series of bright yellow rings stretched exactly down the center of the wall, seemingly at random. The rings were different shapes and sizes. At places they were tangled together, and at places they were more sparse. The pattern, or whatever it was, was echoed on the opposite wall.

The effect was like someone had stretched a measure of chaos in a perfectly encased line on either side of us.

I stepped out, and immediately regretted it.

My legs and shoulder swerved down onto the wall next to me, followed by my arms, hip, and forehead. I gasped, pushing against the wall, but the wall pushed back. I felt dizzy.

"Wait a minute," I said, electing to cling to my current spot for a bit. "Is this—is this the floor?"

"It is indeed." Isaiah made no effort to hide his amusement. He stepped out into the cubed hallway with perfect confidence to stand next to me. "Rite of passage, baby," he laughed.

"Oh, hysterical. Close the door. I can't get oriented with the other hallway just... *looking* at me like that."

Isaiah complied and waited patiently for me to get my bearings. I thought at first that I should close my eyes in order to reset my point of view, but the result was an intense, sharp nausea, and I popped them open as wide as I could, resolving never to blink again.

"Well, that's new."

"It's an electromagnetic grav gen—"

"Yeah, yeah. There's a grav generator in the floor. *Wall.* Whatever. Kinda figured that one out when I started falling sideways."

116

"Same paragrav tech as the Asian Ark."

I chuckled in spite of myself, remembering our foray into diplomacy beneath the grand deck of the center of that ship. That had been dizzying, too. "I do recall, Ise. Thanks so much for the tactile reminder."

He graciously offered a hand, which I refused with rather less grace, and I tripped on my own forearm as a result. I decided to hug the wall a little longer. No, the floor. "It's a floor now," I said firmly, mostly to myself. "Flooooor."

For some reason, he found this amusing. "Come on, Char. The only way out is through."

I sniffed at him, but accepted his still-outstretched hand, and stood. Now the tangled yellow rings were above and below me.

I took a tentative step, clinging to Isaiah, and felt some of my balance return. "Okay. That's better."

"Nothin' like your first time," he said, gently guiding us forward. "So. This is the Center Sphere. It's made of several blocks, each built with the highest tech Earth had to offer."

"The balls are cities," I began, picturing the whole Ark, "and the spikes are control towers and landing pads." We were moving steadily now, and I released his arm.

"Some of them may be weaponized. We're not sure."

"Oh, I think we can be pretty sure," I said dryly. "So what's in the sphere again?"

"Whatever's needed. It's broken down into blocks, like I said. Every block can do almost anything you can think of. They change 'em out when they decide they need to. Here, watch this." We had come to a gap in the floor. It was a perfect cube of empty space. Isaiah backed up a bit, got a running start, and leaped across. "Gotta have a little momentum," he said from the other side. "The very center

117

of the gap is microgravity. Like jumping over a big hole on every side at once."

I shook my head, bemused, and took a few steps back. Then I clenched my fist and, releasing it, catapulted myself across the gap. My stomach dropped, or floated, for the split second I spent at the center of the gap, but by sheer force of will, I landed neatly next to Isaiah.

"Not bad, little bird."

"You don't have to sound so shocked."

He smiled down at me, and I thought for the thousandth time that he had changed in ways I had yet to understand. Then he leaned in close. "Then follow me."

He took off running down the hall, leaping across the next gap. I followed, and he nodded his approval, a devilish glint in his eye.

Not to be outdone, I increased my speed.

That was a mistake, as it turned out. The very next gap we came to, Isaiah didn't jump. Instead, he did some twisty, flighty hop and went directly into the square, alighting easily on the wall of the intersecting hallway.

*No, Char, the floor. Once you land on it, it's a floor.*

Unfortunately for me, this happened about the same time that I reached the edge of the gap, so I went flying past Isaiah, only sideways. I drew my legs in, mid-leap, and attempted to land next to him but got caught in the directional switch of the competing grav generators and made a complete flip.

And then another. And another.

Blast. I flung my legs out, slowing my inertia, and hurled myself toward Isaiah, arms first. Mercifully, this worked, and I flopped onto the deck at his feet like some kind of astonished porpoise.

"Spectacular form," he observed. "I gotta take a few points for that landing, though."

"Shut up." I stood carefully, not letting so much as a finger out of place. Meanwhile, Isaiah did not bother to hide his amusement. I gave him a prim sniff. "Are we going someplace or not? And anytime you want to let me in on the plan would be just great. Do we have somewhere to be, or don't we?"

"We have to be where we are, Char. It's all part of the journey. Although we are awaited, since you ask."

I raised my eyebrows. "Well?"

"Well, what?" he said.

"Well, let's go, then." He laid a hand on the wall near my head, where there was a flat black doorpad I'd somehow missed during my acrobatics routine. It turned yellow at his touch, matching the rings on the floor, and the adjacent wall retracted into itself.

I leaned forward, peering through the doorway, but Isaiah guided me gently through. My foot landed on dried leaves, and I breathed in as the door slid shut. The air was warm and clean, and it smelled like fresh dirt.

*Not dirt*, I corrected myself mentally. *Earth*.

We were surrounded by trees—young pines, saplings—and I thought I heard the sound of flowing water somewhere nearby. I realized that I could not speak. I squeezed Isaiah's arm, full of desperate hope. A thin trail was etched into the burgeoning forest before us. There was only one place this could possibly be.

In response to my mute expression, he smiled, and I felt my face split into a grin so wide it hurt. His voice was deep and cool, and he said the words I'd wanted to hear since I woke from Adam's drug. "Welcome to the biosphere,

119

Charlotte. Someone's been expecting you for quite awhile now."

I raced through the trees without stopping to marvel at the world around me. Dappled light hit the crude earthen trail before me, and the underbrush flicked across my ankles every few steps. I saw birds.

*Birds.*

And squirrels, and I knew without looking, as surely as I could feel my own heartbeat, that there were insects in the trees and worms in the ground. That if I went far enough, I'd be brushing the gossamer remnants of a spider web off my arm or out of my hair.

Isaiah was behind me, but I ran so fast that within moments, I'd lost the sound of his footsteps. I ran faster, unwilling to turn back until the trail hit a clearing, but Isaiah was nowhere to be seen. It didn't matter. I didn't need him to tell me I was exactly where I wanted to be.

The clearing was short, surrounded by the woods on all sides save one, and across the way stood a long row of short houses. The space was lit by a warm yellow light that could almost have been the sun. I took a tentative step into the meadow. When I'd crossed half its length, I was spotted by a boy of about twelve, and as I looked at his face, something pulled against my already-full heart. He cocked his head and ran into a cabin before I could put a name to the feeling.

And then he returned with my brother.

# Fifteen

West was tall, taller than our father. His once-pale neck and face were lightly tanned, and his skinny, fragile aspect had given way to a lean, wiry bulk. He wore simple work pants and a white cotton shirt that was worn but clean. Its sleeves were rolled to the elbow, revealing a similar tan on his hands and forearms.

He saw me at once, and broke into an easy grin, then came bounding across the field toward me, followed by the boy, laughing and shouting all at once. "You made it! You made it!" He punctuated this with a goofy skip, arms wide, every few paces, and I found that I was laughing, too. The first new joke between us. I skipped a few leaps of my own, and then we were together.

He wrapped me in his arms and spun me around until my feet left the ground. "You made it," he said again.

"And so did you," I said, trying to fit this image of West together with my memory of the pale, frightened boy I'd struggled to protect during Adam's fateful attack on the cargo hold of the North American Ark. I couldn't. The thought made me laugh out loud all over again.

"Hey, man," said West. "Say hello."

The boy at his side shuffled a foot and offered me a dimpled grin of his own. "Hey. You're here!"

When I heard his voice, I gasped. "*Maxx?* Good grief! You're—wow. You got so big, buddy." I gave him a hug, and he smiled at me, still shy. We were just about the same height. "Ise!" he said, breaking away. "You got her!"

"I did indeed," said Isaiah. "You got the cards?"

West nodded behind him and began to usher us across the remaining length of the field. "Yeah, back in the house. We better get them on you before the next scan."

I walked as though on a cloud. My brain continued to process each happy revelation a beat slower than it should. "You have a house. And a son."

"Sure do," said West. "And, okay, brace yourself..." he said, letting his tone trail at the end. We reached the door, and he gave me an enigmatic look, then guided me inside.

The cabin was simple. Four walls, a window, and two beds, one lofted above the other. A basic stovetop over a short icer. A rocking chair, a woven mat...

And a crib.

My universe stopped right there, right in that house in the middle of an impossible forest, and redirected itself toward the child before me. Dark brown eyes in a pale, round face, topped off with a rug of thick black hair. Seeing me, she smiled, and I saw all eight teeth in her head, and plenty of gums to spare.

"Easy on the arm," said West, prying my hand off him. "That's my livelihood, you know."

"You're... you have a..."

Without ceremony, West scooped up the child and placed her in my arms, resting her against my hip. Shocked, I wrapped my arms around her. She returned the favor, and my existence was expanded in a thousand ways, all of which crowded into my mind at once, choking me.

When he caught my expression, West seemed to freeze as well, taking in the sight of his daughter in my embrace. "Cecelia," he said, and his voice broke. "That's our Cecelia."

I hunched my back and lowered my head over hers, wrapping myself around her as closely as I could. She was warm and soft, and as long as I lived, I would never let anything happen to her.

"Cecelia," I whispered at last. "It's nice to meet you."

"Put this on," said Isaiah. He looped a plastic-looking chain over my head. It was delicate and white and had a green square, which I hung in front like a charm. "It's a green card. Kind of like a guest pass."

"For the biosphere?" I asked absently. Cecelia rested an arm on top of mine, and I decided to spend the rest of the week squishing its little fat rolls.

"For this part," he said. "There are a few sections open to the public, as long as they stay on the path. Everything else is monitored by body signature. Delicate nature of the ecosystems. Can't have people walking around everywhere." He paused. "I gotta say. It's strange to see you like this, Char."

"Like what?" I asked.

"I don't know. Maternal, or something," said Isaiah.

"Aunt Char," said Cecelia, and I looked at West, my eyes wide.

"She just said—" I started.

"Aunt Char," Cecelia insisted.

"That's your name, right?" West grinned. "We talk about you." The thought made me shake my head in wonder.

"She can *talk*," I said, as though that were the most fascinating thing I'd ever thought of.

"Well. She's a year and a half old," West offered. "She can say a few things. Which makes her a lot more talkative than her brother."

"See ya!" she giggled.

"Hey, I'm not going anywhere," I said, giving her a little bounce.

"No, it's *Ce*-ya," said West. "That's how she says her name."

"I love her," I said firmly. "Aunt-Char-loves-you, Ce-ya," I said gently, directly into Cecelia's face. She returned my solemn gaze, and I turned to Maxx. "And you, too, Maxx Man. I love you, too."

Dinner was lentils and a salad, the best I'd ever had. A light rain had begun to fall, and it pattered against the simple roof of the cabin. I ate delicately, directing my fork around Cecelia, who remained firmly planted in my lap. My mind remained on Eren and my father, but Cecelia seemed as unwilling to part with me as I with her, and as the meal went on, stretched by animated retellings of shared memories, her warm, solid little body relaxed into my other arm, giving the full weight of her head to my shoulder and making me calm, like a heavy blanket on a dark, peaceful night.

Marcela returned halfway through, offering no explanation for how she'd spent the rest of her day, and served herself a bowl, shaking thick drops of rain from her hair. She never let her eyes off her daughter in my arms. She must have decided she approved of the situation, because she sat across from us, between West and Maxx. She kissed West easily on the mouth, a sight I'd yet to get used to, and ruffled Maxx's hair, squeezing the back of his neck. They were the most natural gestures in the world. As they looked at her, she seemed different to my eyes. She fit into the space between them as though they'd been carved around her. She was no less the soldier I'd known her to be, but this was a dimension of her soul I hadn't seen before. Marcela, Wife and Mother.

Just as I admonished myself to stop staring, her eyes met mine. Isaiah was in the middle of the story of our escape from the sick bay, so she simply smiled a greeting. I smiled back, cuddling Cecelia a little closer, and she gave me a nod.

Maybe I belonged here, too.

As always, my happy moment tempered itself almost instantly, and I cleared my throat, stopping the well of pressure that had built up in my chest. Unfortunately, it was a little louder than I'd intended, so I stopped the conversation around me, too. "So. Rain," I said.

My brother nodded. "Started up about a month ago. It comes and goes. Can be kinda unpredictable." He took on a contented look. "Just like back home."

"Better than the old system," said Maxx. "I don't have to run the hydros any more."

"It's easier," West agreed. "Probably takes some getting used to, for some of us." He glanced pointedly at Mars.

"I like to show up for work not soaking wet," she shrugged. "Call me crazy."

"It's only been a few weeks," he said gently. "Give it time."

"Speaking of which," I said. "What have you heard about Dad and Eren?"

Isaiah and Mars exchanged a quick look. "We haven't been able to get them out," said Ise. "But I think we'd know if anything had happened to them."

"I haven't seen your dad at all," said Mars. "That's probably a good sign."

"And Eren?" I asked.

"It's rare," she said carefully. "But it happens. He's fine, Charlotte."

"Fine, how?"

She turned to Isaiah, who shrugged. "Thing is," Mars began, "we don't know. But it looks pretty good. As far as I know, they're not hurting him at all."

I shifted, unsatisfied. That could easily change now that I was no longer around.

"The plan right now is to keep you here," said West. "No one's expecting that green card back. It can't be traced. I don't think they can trace me, either. I got all new papers as a refugee. I've never used my real name here, and neither has Mars. Dad never contacted us. Isaiah would be recognizable, but he uses a different pass every time he visits, and we don't usually meet here at the house. Or even in this biome. Seems pretty clean."

"We're already at Eirenea. They'll probably announce debarking plans any day now, unless they start with the biosphere transfer," said Mars.

Something in her tone made me weigh her words more carefully than West's, but he jumped back in enthusiastically. "We'll see how the new Treaty reads, and then maybe apply for immunity, or a trial, or something. You haven't done anything wrong."

It was a nice plan, a sweet little dream, and they had worked so hard. I didn't have the heart to spoil it. So I nodded, soaking it in for as long as I could. Somewhere over the forest, the rain increased its intensity.

When we'd finished eating, Maxx went to sleep, and we

sat on the front deck of the house in the gathering darkness, sipping hot tea from clay mugs. I peppered the others with questions. I was starving for information. What was their life like? How had they gotten here?

It turned out that West had taken four years to qualify for a post in the biosphere, but it was his as long as he wanted. "The work is hard," he explained, "but everyone wants in anyway. I spend most of the day tending to the biome—this is the Deciduous Biome, by the way; we have four others in the 'sphere—but I also have to produce ground-breaking research every so often. Pun intended." He snickered at his own joke, and Mars rolled her eyes to me good-naturedly. I had to laugh.

"Maxx has ed and training for most of the day, and Mars is always at the sick bay. We qualified for refugee status immediately, thanks to Adam's psychotic tendencies, and they were happy to have an Academy-trained doctor, so for a long time, we lived in general housing, in the city dorms. It's not the worst, but it's crowded. Maxx had to sleep on the floor. I couldn't even work in maintenance. Those guys have a PhD in engineering, minimum. I wasn't qualified to teach preschool up here. If she hadn't married me, I don't know where I would have ended up."

"Straight out the airlock with the rest of the rabble," said Mars.

"She jokes," he said, "but without her, I'd have been boxing lunches and soap rations in the hull for the rest of my life. Maxx, too."

"Better than the alternative," I said, but West shook his head.

"Not to me," he said seriously. "They put you in a tiny room for twelve hours a day, and it's all crowded with supplies. Everything shakes whenever the grav generators adjust to the acceleration. I was having attacks a few times a week. It got bad. I stopped eating, couldn't sleep. I honestly didn't think I would make it."

"The Lightness?" I asked.

He nodded. "She'd wake me up from the spells by reading me biotech research and making me study for the next boards. I failed so many times, but she'd just sign me up for the next one. She never quit."

I looked at Mars, expecting another joke, but her face was serious as she gazed at my brother. "Neither did you," she said quietly. "You're stronger than you think."

My throat was tight, and my niece was warmly nested in my arms. West was fine. He'd never needed me, anyway. In many ways, he was better off without me, same as always. It was a strange feeling—something like relief, but much harder to swallow.

My brother's family belonged here, by right of accomplishment. I did not.

Even if I could clear my name, I'd missed several years of regular, doomed-to-die-in-a-meteor school back on Earth. No amount of biotech papers could ever possibly catch me up. The last time I'd set foot in an elite institution, the War dominated the news, and daily life had been tragically easy to take for granted. We hadn't been trained for survival in space at all. No one around me even knew about the meteor. I was barely ten years old, with no criminal record.

I would never, ever be good enough to live here.

"How did you leave it with Dad?" I asked.

"He decided to stay," said West, his voice distant. "It all happened so fast. He was getting on the hopper, then he jumped back. Told Mars to get in the pilot's seat. He said he couldn't leave you."

His words hung in the air, and the rain pressed in from outside, making the space inside the cabin brighter. Sacred.

My father hadn't left me. I pulled Cecelia closer and blinked a few times. Her hand rested on the end of my arm, where my hand should have been.

"None of us wanted to," Mars added. "I had to make them safe."

"You didn't have a choice," I said quietly. "I can't even think about the things Adam would have done if you stayed. I'd have been so mad at you."

She nodded solemnly. "He had it in for all of us. Didn't make it any easier."

West was staring through the open doorway. The rain broke, and the tops of the trees were again visible from the table. "Dad shook my hand. He looked me in the eye and told me he loved me. He said he was sorry. It was so weird, Charlotte. I told him I was too, and he said he'd never lose hope of seeing me again. And that was it." He dug his thumb into a knot on the wooden deck. "All that time I spent being angry, and now he's gone."

"We didn't give up on seeing you, either," said Mars. "We knew you had Eren."

"I thought he might have turned, actually," said Isaiah. "I couldn't get anything through to him." In general, the Remnant had never trusted Eren, the son of their greatest enemy, and Mars and Isaiah were no exception.

"I wondered about that myself not too long ago," I said. "Turned out to be a very convincing scheme to keep Adam from killing me. A little too convincing for my taste, if I'm honest. Apparently, he'd decided that keeping me in deep stasis was better than risking death."

"He decided right," said West firmly. Mars didn't look so sure. "We're here now, Char. We made it across the sky. They'll forgive you for escaping."

"That's actually true," said Mars. "We just have to convince them you were innocent with Ark Five."

"Why not just leave me in prison, then?" I asked.

Three sets of eyes looked at me like I was crazy.

"I mean, I'm so glad you didn't. I wouldn't give up this night for anything. But if we were already at Eirenea, and I was already presumed innocent—"

"You didn't know?" Mars asked. Her voice was more gentle than usual. Which was irritating. I didn't need her pity.

"Know what?"

"They were planning to torture you, more and more, until you cracked. They passed some kind of special resolution about it a few weeks ago. Sacrifice the one life in the hopes of saving a whole lot more. I mean—" she added hastily—"that was their plan."

"And we couldn't have that," Isaiah said frankly.

"We got to work as soon as we could," said Mars. "We couldn't stop the first few rounds, but we were able to get you out before they escalated."

"They were never going to stop, not ever," West added grimly.

Something finally clicked together in my mind. "The first rounds?" I said. "I *was* drugged. I knew it."

"According to what I could find, you were," said Mars. "Not quite a hallucinogen, but enough of a punch to put you out of your mind a little. They just wanted to get you to talk, at first. Trippy stuff."

"She found a way to get on the team in charge of monitoring your vitals," said Ise. "Smart girl."

West smiled at her adoringly. It should have irritated me, but this time, it didn't bother me at all. I hoped I could always remember them exactly like this. Together, happy. In love.

"If you'd confessed right then, they'd have stopped. Held a trial. But you didn't, so the plan was to keep going," Ise told me.

"Until I *died*?"

"Or confessed," he said.

"But I couldn't confess. I didn't do anything."

"That's what we're telling you. They decided to eliminate the *possibility*. Get as much as they could out of you, for the greater good. Char, they lost an *Ark*. It's unforgivable. But I understand."

My hands went cold. I stood suddenly, jarring Cecelia. She woke and began to fuss. "Oh, no. Oh, no," I said. "They still have Eren."

Mars bit a lip, and I had the sense that I was finally catching up to the rest of the group. "Not exactly," she said. "I mean, they do, but they don't. I knocked him out. He's in stasis."

"You *WHAT?*" I said, prompting a full-on cry from Cecelia. "Sorry, sorry," I whispered. The night sky seemed to redden before my eyes. I couldn't believe I'd trusted her for one minute.

"I had no choice." Mars stood, lifting her hands in a surrendering gesture. "If they drug him enough, he'll tell them our names, and they will come for us." She indicated Cecelia. "All of us. But this way, they can't hurt him. He's safe. We're all safe."

131

I was never safe. Not ever. "Until they get the antidote," I said, jaw clenched.

"They'll never suspect me. They'd have to find Adam first," she said. "Or they'll have to figure out a million things he's known for years."

"How did you...?" I shook my head at her. My anger was dissipating, but in its place, I felt a gaping sense of despair.

"The stasis drug? I stole it from him years ago, along with the antidote, when we worked together in the Remnant. Before he started blowing stuff up. Just in case."

I blinked. "Just in case."

"I like to be prepared." She shrugged, taking Cecelia from my arms. "You are here. We are safe. I don't have anything more to say about it. Good night."

West stood up too, disliking the tension, but wanting to follow his wife. "G'night, Char. We'll talk tomorrow. It's so good you're here."

"Goodnight," I said at last, my despair hardening into resolve. "And Mars. Thank you."

The night air was cold after the rain. I sat next to my old friend Isaiah under a starless sky, mere feet from my family, and wished the moment could go on forever. I felt safe, happy.

And that feeling never lasted.

We were not in a forest, deep in the woods of Earth. We were in space, surrounded by a ship. And ships could be sunk.

Still, the darkness gathered around us, and I felt secure for the moment. I'd missed so much. I hoped that in time, our years of separation would lose their bite. My family had been waiting for me here. Isaiah had come for me. My father had never left the North American Ark.

Eren had never left my side.

"How long since they fixed your eyes?" I asked abruptly.

"'Bout three years back. I have Mars to thank for that. She'd been studying the system since we got here. Once she infiltrated the medical wing, we had access to all the equipment. She built a team—on the level, by the way—and they fixed me right up." He smiled again, an easy smile, and I wondered if there weren't other changes I had yet to pick up on.

"On the level, huh? Seems like she fits in here. Belongs."

He nodded. "They all do. Look at 'em."

His melancholy hung in the air between us, creating a companionable silence. "So Mars became a doctor. West became a farmer. What about you?" I asked him. "Where have you been?"

"Oh, the boxing rooms aren't so bad," he said, his tone blending with the night air.

"But you like the dorms? Better than prison, anyway."

"I didn't qualify for housing. They take the refugees, they give you food. You work when a spot opens. It keeps the madness away. But they can't house everyone. The Ark was full when it took off."

Isaiah was one of the smartest people I'd known. "Surely if you—"

"Char, baby. I've spent twelve years of my life in prison, where we barely went to class, and I wasn't all that old to begin with. Half of that I spent learning how to *read*, once my sight was gone. Maybe if things had gone another way, I could have trained to be a teacher, or worked in the government. I'd have liked that. Even working with

133

Guardians. And maybe I *did* matter up here, almost. But that was a different life, and it's time for me to count my blessings. You could stand to do the same."

"But, after everything. The Remnant. You were a *king*."

"The Remnant is gone. And maybe that's the way it was always meant to be." Isaiah's words were soft, but his jaw was tight, and his silver eyes seemed to blaze in the moonlight. "I did what I came to do, Charlotte. Your family are citizens. I have kept my promises to you."

I knew his pain wasn't directed at me, but it burned anyway. It made me bitter. "It's not over. None of this is over. We made it, Isaiah. We got all the way to Eirenea. But we'll never make planetfall while Adam is out there. Look, we're still alive. That has to count for something."

"It counts. Enough that I don't take it for granted." He shook his head, as though he couldn't believe how naïve I was. "Doesn't it scare you that no one's tried to stop him? Peace at any cost. Did you expect me to bring you an army?"

In the silence that followed, I wrapped my mind around my next move. As long as Adam was out there, this Ark wasn't safe, and neither was mine. And as long as my father was out there, I would never stop trying to find him. I wouldn't abandon Eren, either, even though I didn't doubt that Marcela had hit her mark. They wouldn't hurt his body. His mind would be enslaved, tortured. But he would remain alive.

I glanced back at the cabin, at my sleeping family. I would make them safe if it was the last thing I ever did.

And then I looked at Isaiah. "So you won't come with me. You won't fight."

Isaiah regarded me calmly. "My daddy died in the War. They called him a hero, and I suppose he was. Didn't make

134

much difference though, did it?" I finally recognized the anger underneath his words. I think it had been there all along, but I hadn't known him as well as I thought. I hadn't heard it until now, and now that I heard it, it was a part of every word.

"I think about him sometimes," he continued softly. "I wonder what he would think of me. My mother lived with her grief, but at least she knew the War was over. Then we get up here, and people still just want to fight. So I did what I could." He was quiet for a moment. "I'm not a king, Char. Never was. But I made a difference for a little while.

"All that's over now. It came to nothing, just like how my daddy died. It's the end of the road." His arms reached for mine, but I saw in his eyes that he knew my mind already. His tone went down a pitch, pleading. "Stay with me here among the trees. Let's just enjoy the journey together."

I'd always loved his voice, mellow and deep. There had been a time when I'd have followed him almost anywhere. In another life, he was still young. He'd never grown stubborn or jaded. He'd never broken.

In another life, we could have loved each other differently. Better.

But I couldn't fix him, and none of us could change the past. All I could do was press forward. I set my voice to steel and pulled free of his embrace.

I was going to find Adam. My brother would grow old, his feet planted in a real forest. He would watch his children grow.

My life could still count for that much.

"Goodbye, Isaiah."

He nodded, silent, and watched as I started across the small field. I looked back once before disappearing into the trees. Isaiah sat motionless in the moonlight, exactly as I'd left him, his silver eyes following me.

The trail ahead was dark and thorny, but it couldn't go on forever. I braced myself and entered the forest.

When I reached the edge of the biome, the rain had begun anew. This time, it was anything but peaceful. It set me on edge, and I wasn't sure why. Perhaps because I had no sanctuary from it or perhaps because I was cold. I pushed the thought aside and fumbled around for several minutes, glad I still had the green card hanging from my neck. The doorpad had to be around here somewhere. But it was too dark out, and the doorpad was black, as I recalled. At least I wasn't racing against the scanner.

At long last, it activated, and the door slid open, retracting into the wall of the cube. "Huh," I muttered. I was several feet away from it. I hopped back down the wall, keeping a hand against the flat plastic panels. Rain slid around my hand and down into the earth below. I ducked, feeling the water run down my back, and sped up. Why had they put the panel so far from the door?

"Hey," hissed a voice, causing me to jump nearly out from under my own scalp.

"Aagh," I scream-whispered. "Isaiah? *West?*"

"It's me," said Mars, her scarlet hair visible among the trees in the starlight. "Stop with the names already."

"Mar—sorry. What on earth—"

"Please," she said. "Like you could do this by yourself."

I grimaced. "You belong back there. With them."

"I have as much to lose as you. And besides. You can't even open the door." Her smirk glinted in the light from the hall. "Don't act like you don't need me."

"Wouldn't dream of it," I said, my mind flitting back and forth between dread and something lighter. Relief, perhaps. I wasn't alone after all. "So. It's one last adventure. For old times' sake."

"Let's go save the ships," she said grimly. "Let's go end this."

# Sixteen

I managed to leap over the micrograv spaces without embarrassing myself too much, and Mars looked at me as we reached the end of the maze of blue, cubed hallways.

"Where to?" she asked. "What's the plan?"

I cleared my throat. "I, uh, don't have a whole plan just yet. But I think I know how to defeat Adam. And I think I know where he's going, too."

She nodded approvingly. "And?"

"Well, I think he's with An. He can't have gone back to the North American Ark. We'd have heard about it."

"There's always Ark Four. Maybe he went there."

I shook my head. "They're unarmed, and Europe wants him dead. If he wants to avoid capture, he's going to need weapons. An army. The Asian Ark's the only place he could get that now."

"So we hijack a hopper? The Asian Ark is impenetrable," she said flatly. "That will never work."

"Oh hey, thanks for the confidence, but no. I think our best move would be to contact An. See if she's willing to give him up. At the very least, we can warn her about him."

Mars weighed that idea. "She's not exactly reliable."

"She's reliable in her way. We know she's ruthless. She wants to preserve the peace as long as possible. But if there's a fight, she will make sure she can win. I'm betting Adam makes her nervous."

She sighed. "We'd have to find the comm room. I'm pretty sure it's all in French, though. Do you speak French?"

"No. Do you?"

She shook her head. "Okay," she said, her voice determined. "Do you know where it is?"

"No," I said. "Do you?"

"No. What makes you so sure she'll even speak to you?"

The truth was that I wasn't sure of anything. But An and I had a strange connection. We understood each other. Something told me that if I found a way to reach her, she'd give me a shot. I couldn't explain all that to Mars, so I gave her an apologetic look instead.

She scoffed. "The rumors of your abilities have been greatly exaggerated."

"Not helping. Besides, that's not the first step anyway."

"What is the first step, then?"

I couldn't help smiling a little. "It *was* going to involve breaking into your office. So."

She narrowed her eyes. "What for? Wait, no. You want the antidote." Her voice sped up as she pieced together my thoughts. "You think we're going to go rescue your boyfriend. He's safe where he is. That is a terrible plan."

"First of all, no it's not. And second, you're here now. So obviously, we're not *breaking* in."

She sucked her teeth, glanced around the corridor. "Look," she said, her voice softer. "I know you care about him. But my antidote is an older version. When he wakes up, he'll be… less than functional. It's a lot of extra risk, and he'll probably be dead weight."

"Nevertheless. We're getting Eren first." I crossed my arms.

She shook her head. "I'd get caught, be exposed."

"None of that will matter if we don't stop Adam. We need Eren, Mars. He's good at preventing major wars, which is pretty key here. I mean, he trained as a diplomat. He's an expert with the comm systems, and he speaks French. At least, I'm pretty sure he does." I stopped, giving her time to fully roll her eyes. "But none of that is what really matters."

There was a long pause before she threw a hand in the air. "Fine. Astonish me."

I couldn't help my grin. "He's wearing a k-band."

She weighed the idea as though tasting it, tilting her head back and forth. Finally, she nodded. "It's doable. Not easy, of course. But doable."

An hour later, I was hiding in a med supply closet, wondering what was taking so long, when the door sucked open and Mars flung herself in. "Hey," she hissed. "Where are you?"

I moved the pile of sturdy white linens I'd carefully arranged in front of my body and emerged from underneath a shelf. When it came to hiding, I took my work seriously.

Mars looked at me like I'd spent the time painting myself purple. "You get a good nap?"

"You laugh, but if someone came in here for supplies, they'd never have seen me," I said archly. "Did you get the antidote? You sure you weren't followed?" I moved to brace the door.

She held up a small object wrapped in a black swatch of fabric. "Here's the deal. The shift change is in ten minutes, but the timing's going to be tight. If the new doctor shows up during the transfer, the current one will know I'm not on duty."

I looked at her blankly. "You need to be on duty? It's a heist, Mars."

"I need to access the screen with the patient manifest. That way, I can order his room unlocked for treatment. So you'll have to distract the incoming doctor while I get the other one to transfer the screen to me."

I shrugged. "Makes sense."

"That's not the hard part. Eren's going to come out of stasis right when the alarms start going off. All of them."

"Okay. So we'll run."

"Still not the hard part. When he wakes up, Adam will know. He's probably monitoring the k-band. He might try to attack the ship."

"So we'll run *fast*."

"Char. Stop to think for one second. Where are we supposed to run *to*? We can't take a k-band back to the biosphere, and you have no one. No one."

I put a hand on her shoulder. "We have to warn An. We have to get her to capture Adam and betray him. Nothing else matters." I didn't add that our chances of convincing An were slim at best, and if we failed, they'd both want us dead. An and Adam were as different as ice and steel, but you could cut yourself on either. The one thing Adam could offer her was the only thing she really wanted: stability. As long as he kept his hands off her Ark and prevented everyone from fighting—and getting grabby with the nukes—on board ours, she was probably willing to work with him.

Mars looked at me for a long moment before nodding. "All right. Wish me luck."

Wearing a set of uniform scrubs freshly stolen from the supply closet, I felt my skin come alive. It was good to have a job to do. The new doctor was predictably punctual, but he looked to be an easy target, stopping to give pre-round orders to the first nurse he saw.

Which was me.

"I'll need all the scans from yesterday and an update on the Read lady. Has the coffee come through yet? Where's the other doctor?"

I looked at him. "My shift hasn't started yet. I got five more minutes."

"Close enough. Let's get going. They'll be diverting staff to the secure areas again today."

I gave a slow nod at the clock above the door. "Four minutes, now."

The doctor seemed briefly at a loss before deciding he was angry. "Listen here. I don't give a single blinking ion what kind of shop they ran on your last assignment, but we're not here to play around. There's a list as long as your arm of people who want your job."

"You wanna write me up? Go ahead. I'm not clocked in. I can't even access the reports yet. You asking me to steal them? I'll let you explain to the board why you didn't take protocol seriously."

He opened his hands in a show of shock. "What are you doing standing around if you haven't even clocked in yet?"

I leaned against the wall. "You know, my last super tried to get me to work off-hours. He's shipping band aids now."

"Are you threatening me?" He took a step closer, clearly

expecting me to shrink back. I didn't budge. "Let me put it this way. The review board takes my comments under *special* advisement. So if I were you, I'd get moving."

"Sure thing, doc. In three-and-a-half more minutes."

He scoffed, and finally threw up his hands. "You people think you're above everything. Let me know how that works out for you at your next placement." He turned to blast through the door.

"Wait!" I said quickly. The note of panic wasn't entirely fake. "I have children!"

He didn't look back. "Should'a thought of that before mouthing off to a shift super."

"Look!" I put a hand on his shoulder, stopping him. "I just needed a break! Five minutes without them screaming at me and tearing up the condo after I spent all morning cleaning it," I said, echoing something I'd heard a juvy instructor say on more than one occasion. "Five minutes to myself, before work started! Don't you have kids?"

"No."

"Well, it's not easy." I let my chin quiver. "My shift hadn't even *started* yet."

He groaned. I doubled down, chewing my cheek until I felt my eyes well up.

"All right, all right," he said finally. "Look, don't cry. You really shouldn't have— Stop crying. We'll start over. Name?"

"Magda," I said.

"Magda. Could you please—" he glanced at the clock pointedly—"get clocked in. And then bring me the report on Ms. Read."

I sniffed. "You still want the scans?"

"That would be ideal." He turned to leave.

"Wait!" I said.

With the air of a man of unending patience, he paused heavily. "Yes?"

"What about the coffee?"

At that moment, Mars appeared behind him. She was only partially supporting Eren. His shoulders slumped, and as I watched them, he swayed hard to one side. Mars yanked him upright and, seeing us, gave me a panicked look.

"Let's—let's get coffee," I said to the doctor. "Right now."

"Miss Magda. As I've attempted to impress upon you, I have work to do."

I grinned at him sheepishly. "Not for another ninety seconds, you don't."

At this, he laughed. "Tell you what. You go. Bring me back a cup. We all need a break sometimes."

My look of surprise was genuine. Beyond him, Mars was lunging into Eren, forcing him to swerve into the supply closet. The door closed. I breathed a sigh of relief, to the satisfaction of the doctor. "Okay. Thank you."

"You're welcome," he said magnanimously, and disappeared into the sick bay.

"Is he okay?" I said, crowding into the darkened supply room. "Is he coherent?"

"He is," came Eren's voice. "But not one hundred times. Percent," he corrected himself sloppily. "Definitely not one hundred percent."

"O-kay," I said slowly. "So how was stasis?"

"Not as fun as you made it look," said Eren. "Way more nightmare-y. Where are we? I'm not still dreaming, am I?"

"Nightmarey?" I said. "Wait. *Fun?!*"

"Kidding," he said. I could hear his smile.

144

"I didn't tell her that part," said Mars, "and we are on the EuroArk."

He looked at me, thoroughly confused. "It's a long story," I said.

"But anyway," said Mars. "*An*. How do we get in touch with her again, exactly?"

"You want An?" said Eren. "For what? Doesn't she usually just blow stuff up?"

"For Adam," I said. "We think that's where he went. What's all this about nightmares?"

"It's not important," Mars said quickly. "An."

"Nightmares," I said flatly.

"I may have used an older version of the stasis serum that gives the victim nightmares. Night terrors. I didn't know." She looked at Eren in the near-darkness. "I'm sorry."

"Oh, Eren." I took his hand.

"I would have dreamed about you anyway," he said. "Although I'd have preferred a more pleasant setting."

"That's—that's weirdly touching, Eren." Lightning fast, I ran through the details of how we'd gotten there. The explosion, our imprisonment, and my interrogation. When I told him my theory that Five might still be out there, he nodded.

But when it was his turn to speak, I realized he was still fuzzy from the serum. "I keep thinking of the ways we missed each other," he said. "Like when you traded yourself to the Remnant for me. And then I missed you when you were in stasis. When I find Adam…" he trailed off, then traded that thought for another. "I don't know where we'll go from here," he said. "You and me. But at least we'll be together."

I thought of my family, hidden in the trees, and of the

weight of Eren's head in my lap, and I wondered if I'd ever have to choose between them. My breath came lighter. "That's... sweet."

"*That* is a liability," said Mars, taking in his unbalanced posture. "We have work to do. Next step. We gotta get An on the line."

I squeezed Eren's hand, then reached across him to grab the band on his other wrist. I pressed a few buttons, hoping it hadn't run out of batteries, or whatever it ran on. "An? Are you there?"

Eren leaned down, monkeying me. "An!"

"Maybe she isn't monitoring him."

I snorted. "Maybe when we get to Eirenea we'll find flying salamanders who live in cupcakes."

Mars gave me a long look.

"Sorry. But it's not likely, is what I'm saying." I squeezed the band again, rubbing it. Trying to find an "on" switch. "An! We know you're there. We know you're listening. We're out of stasis. Adam is coming for your Ark next. You'd be a fool to let him in."

Silence.

"You didn't already let him in, did you? Okay," I said, my tone conciliatory. "You're not a fool. But seriously, talk to us. Please. We only want to help."

We looked at each other in the darkness. The band gave no response.

"I told you this was a bad plan," said Mars.

"Not *helpful*," I hissed.

"She's probably already under," she said.

"She's not. She's too smart to let him get that close. It's a fine plan." Even I could tell that my tone was unconvincing.

"It's been a month," said Mars.

"Yeah," I said. "And we'd probably know something if... you know."

Mars rolled her eyes. Again. "Not if he's controlling her. He's totally there."

"He's... okay. He's probably there. Maybe. That doesn't mean she let him..." I couldn't finish the thought. The others looked at me. "All right. So what's our next move, then?"

"Wait for the inevitable?" said Mars. "Hope for the best?"

"I guess we better go with your first idea."

"Which was?" she asked.

"Hijacking a hopper."

"You listen to me," Mars said. "I don't want Adam getting a hold of nukes any more than you do. But we are *not* about to go rescue the Imperial of the Asian Ark. For all we know, she and Adam are best friends, and everything is peachy."

"She doesn't have best friends, and neither does he." I rubbed my face across my bad arm and groaned. I'd lived to see another day, but for what? I was no closer to stopping Adam. It was a matter of time before he slaved the Asian Ark to his programs. "Look. We have to warn An. If he gets close enough to her, he *will* put her in stasis. Then he'll have control of her nukes. Her entire ship. I mean, heck. Maybe she already is."

"We need a better *plan*," Mars said.

"*Well I'm all ears.*"

We locked eyes, and Eren looked from one of us to the other in the darkness. At last, Mars looked away, irritated.

"While I appreciate your concern, Lieutenant Everest," came a voice, "I can assure you that I am *not* in stasis."

# Seventeen

We jumped in unison, and I grabbed Eren by the wrist, lifting his k-band to my mouth. "An? Oh, thank goodness."

"A strange salutation, Lieutenant. I trust you are well."

"I've been worse," I said quickly. "Listen. Adam. You can't take him in. Don't give him sanctuary."

There was a pause as the woman on the other end of the line considered my warning. "Putting aside your tone, Lieutenant, let us consider your position. Why are you asking this of me?"

"Adam is a threat to you as much as anyone. He's not safe. Turn him over to the EuroArk and preserve the peace."

"I like to think I can decide such matters for myself." I pictured a delicate set of eyebrows raising slightly.

"Surely you agree with me, though."

There was another pause. The silence was maddening, but I gritted my teeth until she spoke again. "I am prepared to do as you ask," she said at last. "Provided that you do something for me in exchange."

I exchanged a glance with Mars. "What could I possibly have to offer you?"

"You had an audience with the leadership of the EuroArk.

I find myself in awe of you, Charlotte Turner. Is there anyone to whom you do not have access?"

Mars' expression was dark, and I felt my own face twist. How could An have known that? "Sounds like you're the one with access," I said cautiously. "It wasn't exactly voluntary. I've been their prisoner for weeks. They were planning to tort—" I cut myself short. All I needed was for An to start thinking I had some top-secret info as well. "Why don't *you* tell me how the meeting went?"

"I am happy to make a guess. You refused to tell them about Ark Five," said An.

I shoved Eren's wrist back into his lap in frustration, then apologized quickly. "You have to be kidding me."

"Allow me to convince you otherwise. I know what Adam is capable of, but his path before the North American coup was obscured. He was young, too young to be a major player yet. Only a few people could have had a hand in the fate of Ark Five. My own resources have convinced me that the leaders of the other Arks are entirely innocent. That is to say, they are ignorant. Which leaves those who have controlled Ark Two. Your Ark."

"I've never had control of anything, An. Least of all an *Ark*."

"Maybe. Maybe not. But you must have found yourself in a strange position, Lieutenant. You had access to the leadership of both factions on the Ark. You are an official representative of the Remnant, and yet you married the son of the High Commander."

"Which was *your idea*," I reminded her. "And I was a prisoner to both," I said, angry. An had forced me to marry Eren in order to secure peace on board the North American Ark. It hadn't exactly helped my relationship with his father.

149

It hadn't helped much of anything, come to think of it. "That's about as far from *access* as it gets. And An. I'm a representative of nothing. There is no Remnant. Not anymore."

"Nevertheless. The Commander is dead. His son is in your company. And while Isaiah has eluded us, well, let me simply observe that he has a way of loosing his secrets in your presence."

I ignored that. I wasn't all that interested in helping An find Ark Five. She was just this side of predictable, and she was dangerous beyond words. If, as I suspected, she was still working with Adam, then who could stand against them? "Adam probably blew it up before we started fighting."

"He lacked the weapons," she said flatly, making it clear that she wasn't falling for that or any other story. "But even if he didn't, they were never deployed. The only traces of radioactivity our scanners have found are from the sun."

I blinked. "Maybe Ark Five's life support glitched, and they all suffocated. Maybe it got hit by one of the meteors that missed Earth. Maybe their rockets broke down before they got going, and they're still sitting back there, right where we left them."

"Then it would have sent out a signal. A ship in distress hails every other Ark automatically. This function cannot be disabled, Lieutenant. We all have an interest in the other Arks."

I closed my eyes and took a breath. The best lies are mostly true. Mostly. "An. I'm telling the truth about this. I always have been. *I don't know what happened to Ark Five.*"

"Oh, now that, I believe."

150

I stared at the band incredulously. "Then how can you possibly expect me to help you?"

"I have taken measure of you, Lieutenant. You are not without your means, nor are you working alone. This is my offer. Find out for me what happened to Ark Five, and I will refuse sanctuary to Adam and extradite him to Europe if they ask."

"If you're smart, you'll do that anyw—"

"And I will help you find your father."

I went cold. "What do you know about my father?"

There was no response.

"An. You can't just do that. If something happened to my dad, you have to tell me."

"Fugitives need hostages," she said sharply. The sudden steel in her voice threw me, cutting off any response I'd have otherwise given, and we endured a moment of tense silence. "Charlotte Turner," she said finally, slowly. Her voice took on a dreamy quality in spite of her inflexibility. "It may surprise you to hear that I was pleased that you survived the years since we met. At times, I have believed that we share similar goals in spite of the discrepancy between our stations. Like you, I am disinclined to sit idly by in the hope that peace will find us. I will never cease to fight for the continued success of my people. We *will* colonize Eirenea. We will grow.

"But to do that, we must eliminate every threat. This journey is a delicate thing. One misstep, and it will end. Prove to me the fate of Ark Five, and I will tell you what you need to know as well."

There was no sound, not even a click, but the conversation was definitely over. I looked from Mars to Eren, rubbing my hand on my scalp and over my eyes. "Uughh," I moaned. "Adam has my father. An has Adam. I'm just a fugitive.

I'm nobody. She probably has a million nukes, all pointed at the other Arks. What can we *possibly* do?"

Mars gave a plaintive glance to the ceiling. "Emotional fortitude of kittens," she muttered.

I scowled at her. "You got any bright ideas?" She glanced down, and I realized I was stroking Eren's still-outstretched arm protectively. It was comforting, somehow, but it wasn't enough. "Because I sure don't. I need to think. Without *this*." I waved at the k-band. "Can you get it off?"

She shook her head. "Aren't you the one who breaks into stuff?"

I stretched my hand across my forehead and rubbed my temples. "Something is just... off." Everything seemed so cut and dried, like it was all laid out ahead of time.

She narrowed her eyes. "Like what?"

*All of it,* I wanted to say. But even I wasn't sure what I meant, so I kept my mouth shut. On the surface, it all fit together. Adam escaped. He had been allied with An in the past, but she was no fool. She was probably keeping a close eye on him. And me.

And everything.

"For one thing," I began, "how did An know about the interrogation?"

"She has spies everywhere," said Mars.

"She's listening to us right now," said Eren. I looked at him, pleased that he was waking up. We exchanged a smile, and I had a sudden moment of clarity.

"Here's another thing. How did Adam kidnap my father?"

"He's... Char, he's *Adam*." Mars rolled her eyes. "If I can get *you* out, he can get to your dad."

I bit a lip. "Maybe," I said. "But he was already gone by then, right?"

"He slaved an entire Ark to his biometrics. Maybe more than one, if we're being blunt," she said. "It wouldn't even be hard for him."

Adam had the capabilities, no doubt. But still. Something was definitely off. "No, you're right," I said.

"Alert the presses."

I made a face at her. "Just—just let me think."

"Try not to pull a muscle," said Mars. She made an open gesture, as if to say *go ahead*, and stopped talking. I had too many questions to sort through, but they were as good a place to start as any. I closed my eyes and picked through them one by one, trying to put a finger on exactly what was bothering me. A few moments later, my eyes popped open.

One question connected all the others.

"Why didn't the panel believe me?" I said aloud, eyeing the k-band. From the beginning, no one could swallow any theory save one: I—or someone like me—had blown up Ark Five. It was as though no other possibility could exist. *Why?*

"We have to talk to Charles," I said firmly.

Mars frowned. "Who?"

"Charles Eiffel. He's some kind of administrator here. One of the architects of the EuroArk. I met him the day I had my big meeting with the Imperial."

"The French guy from the party?" said Eren.

I nodded, and we exchanged another smile, prompting another eye-roll from Mars. "To what end, exactly?" she asked.

"To—you know what? You just have to trust me." I pointed at the band, and she studied it for a moment before capitulating.

"All right, Char. Lead the way."

# Eighteen

I knew a few things about Charles Eiffel. One: he was an optimist. Given the responsibility of choosing which of Earth's great works of art to save from the meteor, he'd scrapped them all and taken in as many babies as he could instead. He'd called it *saving art itself*. Needless to say, he had a certain flair for the dramatic. That's probably why he'd gotten away with it.

Two: His flamboyant personality masked a brilliant mind that understood the risks he took. He'd allied himself with the Remnant in the days before its destruction. We weren't even a legitimate nation, but he'd been on our side anyway, just for the principle of the thing. He could as easily have turned us away, like almost everyone else, and told us we'd all work it out when we got to Eirenea. But he didn't.

I could work with a man like that. Assuming he'd have me.

Not that I had any choice. I was fresh out of queens and commanders. It wasn't like I had any other contacts up my sleeve.

We found our way to his cube within the central sphere without difficulty. If the rest of the EuroArk was well ordered—hallways, spikes, and spheres in a state of perfect discipline—the nursery was anything but. Hundreds of children ran free throughout the vast cube in Charles' command, and I took a moment to appreciate his handiwork. One wall was composed of rows of bunks separated by interior columns of ladders. In lieu of the motivational posters of varying levels of humor I'd always seen in classrooms, paint adorned every spare inch of the walls. Not quite finger painting, but something close. The center of the space had long rows of desks in concentric circles, and there was a series of play areas that looked like they'd been built up from scraps of whatever was handy.

Orderlies dressed in bright colors walked calmly through the crowd, keeping watch over their charges, who played busily. Some painted, some played games. There were blocks and every other tool for creating that I could imagine. A team of pint-sized bikers rode in circles around the perimeter. The far wall of the space was covered in screens. For the moment, the screens were synched to display a composite image of a woman. She smiled down at the scene contentedly. She must be the Mother.

Everywhere—*everywhere*—there was art. The floor was composed of intricate mosaics sloppily pasted together. No, not sloppily, I thought. Just executed by inexperienced craftsmen. On closer inspection, I could see that every shard was painstakingly laid in its place. The walls, as I mentioned, were hand-painted by the students. There was no plain surface among any of the desks, and each bunk was adorned with an elaborate, if crude, quilt. The rungs of the ladders were inscribed with poetry. The lights overhead were hung with pastel filters, and the color and quality of the light vacillated as the filters shifted.

Contrary to my expectations, there were no babies. There wouldn't be, of course, I realized. The youngest of the children would be more than five years old by now. The noises of childhood were everywhere. Singing, shouting, and playing games, and Charles sat at the center of it all, quietly reading a book. I stood and watched a few minutes longer, trying to put a name to my slight sense of discomfort. I could not account for it, save for the obvious: I was an interloper, a fugitive aboard this Ark, and that made me Charles' enemy.

He looked up as we approached.

"Charles!" I stood a few feet away.

He stood in pieces: book down. Hands in lap. Legs and back straightened. We had the attention of the orderlies now, too. From other places around the room, they turned to look at me. When I met an orderly's eye, she returned her focus to her charges. The second time it happened, the skin on my neck began to crawl. By the third, I found myself checking the exits.

But no one came near us, so I took a breath and tried to concentrate.

"Ms. Turner," he said quietly, then smiled. "How good to see you." I blinked. It was as though someone had pulled the corners of his mouth *up*. I was reminded of—

"But not unexpected, judging by your posture," said Mars.

Charles' mouth remained stretched into a smile, and he ignored the question inherent in her statement. "How may I be of service?"

"I—actually, we're here because we—I—thought you might be able to help me," I started uneasily.

"Anything for an old friend."

He sure wasn't acting like we were old friends. But he

wasn't acting hostile, either, so I cleared my throat. First things first. "Got any tin foil?" I asked, trying to keep my tone light.

He nodded to an orderly, who relayed the request to a child in a bright, gentle voice. The girl returned almost instantly with a roll of heavy-duty aluminum... and two more escorts. "Perfect!" I said brightly. She gave me a shy smile and returned to her tasks. The orderlies at her side remained with us. I squeezed the roll between my knees, half-crouching, and tore off a truly massive portion with my good arm as quickly as I could manage, then motioned to Mars to give me a hand.

As Mars leaned in to wrap it around Eren's k-band, his hand slid past her waist. I tilted my head, trying to get a better view, but the movement was too quick. She circled his wrist several times with the tin foil, letting it crinkle a little more than necessary. The sooner we lost contact with An, the better. Still, I couldn't relax. Not yet.

Charles simply watched, immobile.

The children continued to play. The noises of the room were all around us, but either it was my imagination, or they'd gotten a bit quieter since the k-band was wrapped.

Probably my imagination. Eren's hand moved a second time, and I caught a flash of silver. I blinked, then shook my head. His wrist was wrapped in aluminum. Of course I saw silver. My years of running had made me paranoid.

I was just about to address Charles when the orderlies took a step toward us.

All of them. At the same time.

"Charles," I stammered. My pulse began to pick up, but he didn't seem to care or even notice. "This may not be the best time after all. We were just about to leave."

"Were you?" he said, his tone curiously blank.

It happened again. Every orderly in the room took another step toward us. This time, they weren't even trying to hide it. I caught Mars' eye. Her jaw was tight beneath her smile. It was a huge mistake to come here. We were outnumbered eight to one.

If she could handle the orderlies in our group, perhaps I could start moving Eren to the door. I reckoned we'd make it about half the distance before the other ones got us.

Less, if they started running.

I wet my lips. "It's a tr—"

The orderlies nearest us flinched, and I ducked, slamming my fist into the first one as hard as I could. He moved past me, barely fazed, and I realized I was not his target. Eren was.

But the orderly was already too late. Eren's eyes were sharp. Focused. And his gaze was clear.

Perhaps the mistake was theirs.

At a stroke, Eren twisted him backward, then returned his attention to Charles. The remaining orderly gaped, hand to hair, at the syringe that dangled from Charles' thigh. Charles twitched, panicking, and the syringe emptied itself completely.

A flash of black fabric, and Eren was on top of the next orderly. The rest of the room galvanized toward the unfolding fight. It wouldn't last long.

"Marcela. Gun." Eren shot her a pleading look.

Mars pulled a gun from her jacket and aimed it directly at the head of the nearest orderly. He raised his hands, frozen, and the rest of the scrubs in the room ceased their advance.

The room fell quiet, and Eren stood. "Mr. Eiffel," he

said. His voice sounded strong, like it was in my memory, and I gave him an appreciative look. "We'd like to ask you a few questions about Ark Five."

Charles blinked a few times.

Finally, he lifted his head and smiled.

"Ah, the Everests. It *is* good to see you."

As Charles relaxed, so did the orderlies. One by one, they returned their attention to their tasks, shooting careful glances in our direction. Eren gave a pointed look at the ones nearest us, and Charles made a similar face at Marcela. "*That* will need to be confiscated if our conversation is to continue." Eren nodded at her, and after a long moment of consideration, Mars placed her gun in an orderly's outstretched hand. What else could she do? We wouldn't get far if they were chasing us, and it's not like we planned on shooting anyone in cold blood.

Charles waved them away and took his seat.

I was about to launch into an explanation of what we were doing there when Eren cut me off. "Who drugged you?" he said, standing over Charles.

"Drugged?" He shook his head. "I don't know." He gave an enormous shrug, which turned into a stretch, and I had an image of someone just waking up from a nap. "I didn't even know I was drugged."

"Trust me," said Eren dryly. "You were."

"What do you remember?" Mars demanded.

Charles pursed his lips. "Someone came from behind. I am fairly sure of that."

"This can wait," I said, and we filled him in as fast as we could.

"If I understand you," he said at last, standing, "we need

to prove the existence of Ark Five to the Asian Imperial. In exchange, we will take down the monster who destroyed our city?"

We nodded. "We're certainly going to try," said Eren.

"I'm sure you can contact them," I said. "I know what I saw. I know they're out there. Will you help us?"

"Help you contact Ark Five?" Charles asked.

"How do we know she won't attack them?" Mars asked.

"She won't," I said slowly. "They're unarmed, right?" The others nodded. "Surely she'll want to save her nukes for the ones that can fight back."

"You're assuming she has to choose between them," said Charles. "She doesn't."

"How many nukes does she have?" I asked.

"Enough to do anything she wants," he said calmly.

"My impression of An is that she only wants peace," said Eren.

"Control," said Charles. I looked at him. "She wants control," he said. "She will use it to ensure that there is peace."

"Either way, I'm in," I said, clenching and unclenching my fist. So many things weren't adding up, but all I could think was, *Hang on, Dad. I'm coming for you.* "Don't you want Adam under control? We can still beat him. But we need your help. And An's."

"Well, then," said Charles, "we should go."

The comms room required a retinal scan, voice clearance, and the use of Charles' badge. "Why don't they just take a blood sample, while we're at it?" I muttered.

"Don't give them any ideas," said Mars.

"The receiver will take two minutes to unfurl," he said.

160

"If there has been any message from Ark Five, we should be able to pick it up."

I decided to spend the time looking around the room. Unlike the amphitheater that housed North America's communications control, the comm center here had only a few desks. But the desks they had were magnificent: dark green, with enormous, curved-glass shields around each station. They were arranged like blocks around a center square, which also appeared to be made of glass. "Let me guess," said Mars. "One place for everyone on the Council." She was clearly impressed by the set-up in spite of her usual nonchalance.

"I've heard about this," said Eren. "Apparently, you can control the glass's capabilities." He laid a hand on one imposing shield. "It can be opaque or not, and it can block sound and host images as well."

"One station might not even know what the other is up to," I mused, and Charles gave me a quick glance before turning back to the transmitter.

"Ah, success," he said moments later. "I hope this is to her satisfaction." He twisted a knob, throwing the transmission to the middle block.

The center of the room lit up above the square glass pedestal, and a series of metallic taps filled the air. "Morse code," I said quietly. Mars scrambled for a screen and a stem, but Eren held up a hand, his head cocked.

"Hold for translation," he said softly. "*Message reçu. Dispositif... d'invisibilité engagé jusqu'à nouvel avis. Nous avons atteint... la terre. Première mission accomplie.*"

I shook my head, eyes wide. "And that means?"

Eren's brow furrowed over intense blue eyes. "Message received. Cloak engaged until further notice. We have reached... the ground? First mission—" he looked at Charles—"a success." Eren set his jaw, and his gaze met mine. "The message repeats from there. It's on some kind of loop. No telling how long they've been broadcasting it."

I stared at the screen in disbelief. "They reached the ground? Like, Eirenea? You guys, this is huge. They made planetfall! Why are they hiding it?"

Eren shook his head. "The phrasing just sounds wrong. But I'm not sure. And what's all this about a mission?" he asked Charles.

"We shouldn't stay too long," he said, busying himself with another set of controls.

"It's huge, all right." Mars was frowning at a set of calculations on the screen. "But the trajectory doesn't fit. Maybe it's a code? Do we have enough data to pin down an origin point?"

"It's several AU away." Eren turned to the display. "No way it's coming from Eirenea."

"They could have some kind of phantom routing," Mars said.

He shook his head. "It's not like they're trying to hide. They're not even changing frequencies. It's almost like... they're shouting."

"If that were true, they wouldn't use a cloaking device," Mars said, frustrated.

"AU?" I blinked, trying to keep up, but none of it made much sense. "Should we ping them back?"

"Astronomical units, and no. *No,*" said Eren. "We need to stop for a minute. We don't want to draw them out any further until we know what's going on. Remember their last conversation."

I did. Granted, I'd only heard one side of it, but they'd

seemed a good deal more skittish back then. I flipped through the controls on the desk, looking for a line to the Asian Ark. I wasn't sure what I'd do if I found it, though. "In that case, it seems like we shouldn't be announcing anything to An, either. Maybe it's hiding from *her*." I turned back to the desk and started flipping as many switches as I could, but nothing happened. Was it possible that they were all keyed to someone else's fingerprints? "At some point, this is just *paranoid*."

"Not if they think she's trying to kill them," said Mars.

"No, not the Ark. The desk. I need to talk to An," I said, checking under the panel for some kind of failswitch. "I keep thinking we're getting somewhere, but all I have is more questions."

"See, I feel like we need to talk about this *before* we send it to An," said Mars. From the sound of things, she was ducking behind another desk, trying to crack the same system as me. "Surely there's something else we can do? Like, anything else?"

I thought about that. "We could ping the North American Ark." They looked at me. "I mean, I don't think he's there. I think he's probably with An. But just in case."

"You could," said Charles, "but it won't do any good. They went dark some time ago."

"Dark?" Mars said.

"Nothing in or out. No hoppers, no cargo ships. Nothing," Charles explained. "They won't even receive a transmission."

"You're kidding," I said.

"I'm afraid not, my dear," he answered. Something about his tone set me off-balance for the hundredth time that day.

I bit a lip. "Fine. Show me."

Charles pulled up a graphic, and the familiar shape of

163

the North American Ark came into view. "Home sweet home," I said.

"Here's their signal," Charles explained, pointing. "You can see that it's coming across every frequency. Here are the receptors," he indicated a schematic below the graphic, and Eren nodded. "All shut down," he said.

"What's on the signal?" said Mars.

"Happy to play it for you," said Charles. He flipped a switch, and a familiar voice hit the comms.

"To our esteemed colleagues and treasured allies aboard the other Arks," came the message, "we regret that the North American Ark has closed its borders, effective immediately." I inclined my head, listening, and the image of Adam's Lieutenant popped into my mind. I had no doubt that the voice was hers, and that she was no longer under the influence of the drug. There was a certain melancholy to her words that could not have come from a puppet. "This closure is absolute. Any imposition on our airspace, diplomatic or otherwise, will be treated as the gravest of threats to our peaceful existence and an offense to our sovereignty." The voice paused, lowered. "To those who oppose him: our hopes are with you. Good luck."

I looked around the room, but the others were as speechless as I, struck by the finality of the missive.

"The running theory," Charles said, "is that the lady is under his influence. That he is there, consolidating his power."

I shook my head. "The Lieutenant didn't sound like she was drugged," I said. "She sounded genuinely sad. You don't feel sad when you're under. Or anything, for that matter."

"I suppose you'll want to talk to the Imperial," said Charles. Something in his expression put me on guard. I couldn't place a finger on it, though, and I couldn't see a better plan forward, either. I resolved to stay alert.

"You know, that's not a bad plan," said Eren. "Was it just me, or did An seem to be acting strange—stranger than usual—during the conversation?"

"Wait! Did you see that?" said Mars.

"See what?" I asked, my tone level.

"Something moved."

Eren looked around, presumably for a weapon, and said, "Hello? Show yourself. We mean no harm." There was no response.

A shadow moved across the room. We saw it and tensed, as though a cord ran through us all and was suddenly pulled taut. Eren reacted first. I watched, open-mouthed, as he grabbed Charles by the shoulders and threw him to the ground. I should have been moving by then, but I couldn't take my eyes off Charles. At last, it hit me. It was subtle, barely visible. But I was sure it wasn't my imagination. He was *smiling*.

"Get down," Eren shouted.

Now, there was a phrase I'd never needed to hear twice. I ducked into the space below the desk. Mars followed immediately, folding herself beside me in one fluid motion. At the same time, there was a small crash, and the lights went out.

That was not a good sign. In my experience, when someone kills the lights in a room, they are generally more prepared for a fight than the other people in the room.

Mars and I listened, motionless, as Eren and Charles shuffled around for a second. I could barely make out Mars' face, but she seemed to be pointing to the far wall. I strained for any clue as to what might be going on, but all I could hear was the sound of the blood pulsing through my neck.

165

"I really need a gun," I muttered.

"Yeah," Mars whispered, still crouching. She twisted slightly and slid a hand up the leg of her pants, balancing on the ball of her other foot. From there, she unlatched something and withdrew a silver sidearm without a false move. "You really do." She shifted her grip on the gun and slid out into the room.

I made a face at her back.

I needed a weapon, but nothing materialized. Another crash, followed by a hard *pop*, sent a jolt through my body, and my heart pulsed faster. I really, *really* didn't want to be sitting around unarmed when he came for me. I banged my head into the back of the desk in frustration.

A drawer popped open to my left.

*Fancy, fancy.* But of course the people who worked here would have a place to put their stuff while they worked. A quick search of the drawer turned up nothing more exciting than a screen, a stem, and a handkerchief. Like, the kind the old people started carrying around when they outlawed tissue paper during the War. This one had a thin, blocky, red monogram: CBE.

My irritation surprised me. I'd thought I was past caring about the luxuries selected to survive the meteor in place of actual people. After all, it was only a piece of cloth. I braced the screen with a fist and a forearm. And besides, I reasoned, cracking the screen over my thigh, it saved me from using a sock. I selected the longest, most triangular piece of glass from the wrecked screen and, pinning it under my leg, wrapped the handkerchief around the thick part. Then I slid the stem into my sleeve and emerged from the desk in a half-crouch.

The sounds of a fight were to my right, but nothing was

visible at first. Using the desk as cover, I slid my eyes around the room, hoping to catch a trace of movement in my periphery, when the door sucked open. I was too late to stop the intruder, who must not have belonged in the room any more than the rest of us, so I froze, fighting my instinct to hide, and forced myself to focus on the figure making his getaway.

We took stock of each other in the half-light of the hall, and I frowned, confused. But he vanished quickly, knowing I was in no position to give chase. I looked around the room. Charles seemed to have ridden out the skirmish in the same position as I: hiding under a desk. Eren had a small cut on the front of his arm. Mars was bleeding from her lip. She took in my makeshift weapon without changing her expression. Which was angry.

Eren crossed the room to stand next to me, and I gave his hand a squeeze. He seemed fine. For my part, I felt vaguely dizzy.

The three of us turned to Charles. I shifted my grip on the weapon, not quite brandishing it at him. "What do you know about this?"

"Not much," he said casually. Too casually. He stood and faced the group.

Something in his tone set off an alarm in my mind, and all at once, my thoughts came together, and the first of my questions had an answer. *An was never allied with Adam.*

"An wasn't trying to find out what happened to Ark Five, was she?" I asked him. My tone must have set off his alarms, too, because he took a step back. Instinct made me check for his hands, but they were hidden beneath the surface of the square glass pedestal.

"What?" said Mars.

I gave Charles a look hard enough to crack ice. "She was trying to find out what happened to *you*." I turned to the others. "That wasn't Adam who attacked us just now. It was Shan."

"He's a long way from home," Marcela observed, and I had to agree. It was hard to imagine the Asian Imperial's favorite bodyguard anywhere but by her side.

"To be fair," said Eren, taking in my words, "it wasn't much of an attack. More like, we caught him off-guard. Hey, do you guys hear thunder? Are we that close to the biosphere?"

My breath caught as I listened, and a deep, distant rumble weaved itself through the silence in the room. "It's a spaceship, Eren," I whispered, feeling strangely cold. "There's no such thing as thunder." The entire puzzle shifted once again, and the nightmare before us took shape in my mind as the pieces continued falling into place. "And An wasn't just distracted during our conversation," I continued. My voice began to shake, and I lowered my pitch. It didn't help. "She's not getting ready for a fight, is she, Charles? She's already in one."

I turned back to the group. Eren's hands were raised, a determined look on his face. Mars mirrored his posture. Her face was a mask of rage, all of it aimed at Charles. She was actually kind of terrifying when she got like that.

I'd have felt sorry for Charles, if it weren't for the gun he was aiming at me.

"You're working with An," I said, taking in the barrel. I didn't lift my hands. I had no intention of putting him at ease. Not when the world was coming to an end all over again.

"My dear, this entire ship is working with An," he replied calmly. "It's not a fight we can afford to lose."

The last of the questions had an answer, and I was cold. I knew where Adam was. I knew exactly where.

"You don't know what you're dealing with. None of you. I've been wrong all along. Adam never actually escaped." I turned to Mars, struggling to make sense. It was like stepping out into the freezing air in the middle of a hailstorm. "It's not upgraded tech in the biosphere. It's not a fun, easy alternative to the hydro. *It's not rain.*"

She gave me a look halfway between confusion and condescension, until suddenly, understanding set in. Her face went white, and although she was speaking, her lips didn't move. "Oh, no," she whispered. "Oh, no. Oh, no."

# Nineteen

In a flash, Mars was on top of Charles.

Even seeing it happen, I wasn't sure how she did it. But the gun was in her hands, and her face was ablaze with fear and fury.

She was gone from the room before the rest of us got our act together. I ran after her, shouting. "Stop! Just stop! Mars. We have to think this through."

But she barely slowed down. "I have to get to them. I have to make sure they're okay."

"We should have a plan. Mars, please. *He is waiting for us.*"

"I'm sorry, Char," she called over her shoulder. "I am. But I have to get to my children."

I clenched my jaw in frustration. We needed Mars. Not that I blamed her, but I couldn't join her. Not yet. We had to be smart about this. Anything less, and we didn't stand a chance.

I sprinted back into the comms room, fighting a wave of fear and helplessness. But I steeled my spine and squared my shoulders.

"So Adam's here," said Eren. His voice was intense.

170

Powerful. I'm not sure why that surprised me. "On this Ark."

"He's not," said Charles. His calmness was infuriating. "He can't be. It's been weeks. They secured every system as soon as the city blew up. If he were here, we'd know."

I gave him a look. "Oh, like how you knew when he drugged you?"

"Come, Ms. Turner. We both know that was you. Or one of your associates. Adam returned to the North American Ark. His Lieutenant is covering for him."

I shook my head. We didn't have time for this. I had to switch gears. "Where is my father?" We could use him—and whatever was left of his resources—in the coming fight.

"Your father?"

"You know, the guy I got here with?"

He gave me a blank look. "Ms. Turner, the only *guy* you got here with is your husband."

I suppressed the urge to scream. "He was locked up with me for weeks! Surely someone in your position had access to the prisoner manifest."

But Charles just stood there. "I certainly did." He turned to Eren. "Her father was never here."

My lips felt numb. "No, he was there. In the cell." Eren put a hand on my arm, trying to calm me. Oddly enough, it *was* comforting. I jerked away. "No, don't do that! You have to believe me."

"Char," Eren said gently. "You were drugged for five years. It would be normal, at this point, if you—"

"Don't do that." I clamped down on my throat, pressing against the rising knot at its base. It wouldn't help anyone if I broke down now.

"Did you see her father on the hopper?" Charles asked

Eren, who answered with a sharp shake of his head. "Well," he pressed. "Have you seen him at all? Have you seen *Adam* since you got here?"

"I never saw the hopper," said Eren. "I was drugged before we got there." He touched the band on his arm subconsciously. "The goal was to turn Adam over to you. To this Ark. I'm sure he was here."

"You have to believe me," I said, lowering my voice again. "He *is* here. And so is my dad. I can't even fly a hopper, Eren."

"This is preposterous," said Charles. "A hopper doesn't hold four people, Ambassador. She probably engaged the autopilot."

The room went hazy as I bit back tears. I couldn't afford this. *We could not afford this.* Adam was coming. Adam was *here*. What was the play? *Think, Char.*

But I couldn't think. The memory of being drugged, of sliding into nothingness, crowded into my mind. I could not be helpless again. I blocked it out, but it persisted. *What can I possibly, possibly do to stop him?* My cheeks were hot, and I struggled to keep my temper. We had to be strong. We had to—

In a blur, the cube-like chair at Charles' desk hit his enormous shield. The crash and immediate cascade of shattered glass filled the room, jolting us out of our skins. I was nearly as shocked as the others in spite of the fact that I was the one who'd thrown the chair, but I did not pause to survey my handiwork. I did not glance at Eren. There was a time when we had cared about each other openly, but that was long ago, and everything had changed since then. He would never love me again after what I was about to do.

I seized what clarity I could instead. *This is done now,* I thought, scanning the broken glass, *but I'm about to do worse. Forward, Char.*

I grabbed the biggest, longest shard I could and threw myself at Charles. "*Don't* do that," I repeated, my voice strong now. "My dad is here. They both are. I'm not crazy." I raised the edge of the glass to his throat.

Charles lifted his hands. The shock running through my mind played out over his face. It was far from the first time I'd held a weapon, but it was the first time I'd threatened someone's life and meant it. A twinge of regret slipped through me, and I almost dropped the glass.

So I tightened my grip. *Forward.* A thin line of blood appeared at my wrist, sliding out from the fresh cut across my palm, but I felt no pain. Not yet. The smallest drop landed on his perfectly white collar and feathered into a bright, even circle.

"Easy, Charlotte," he said, using my name for the first time. His eyes went to Eren. "A little help, please? Your assistance will be recorded."

I did not turn back to my husband. I couldn't possibly fight them both.

And besides. If Eren were against me, I'd already lost.

"You listen to me, Charles Eiffel," I said, my voice level. "There's a lot you don't know about me, but I can tell you one thing. This is your fight now. And you're going to help me win it."

He was angling toward the desk, casually trying to lean against it, but I pressed into him with my bad arm, keeping the glass at his jugular, and he backed away again. "A friend in need..." he began in a placating tone.

"Is a friend trying to stop a psychopath from blowing

up and killing us all in a fiery wreck," I cut in. "So *sit down*."

To my everlasting shock, Eren turned the cube-chair-thing upright, crunching the glass beneath his boots into the carpet in the process, and offered it to Charles. "Please," he said firmly.

Charles sat.

In the silence that followed, I turned back to Eren. For the briefest of moments, he held my gaze, searching me. His eyes were impossibly blue. "I'm with you," he said simply. "You don't have to look so surprised."

I breathed a sigh of relief. "This wasn't going anywhere without you, you know."

He took in my stance: the weapon, the grip on Charles. The look in my eyes. "Agree to disagree," he said lightly. "What do we do now?"

"Talk to An. We have something she needs." I waved my bad arm at Charles, then frowned at the desk. "It must be fingerprint-locked."

"It is," Eren said, studying the panel. "But we have the fingerprints." He gestured for Charles to come near. "Call her up," he told him. "Throw the comm holo to another shield. Don't try anything clever."

"Wouldn't dream of it," Charles said, tapping a couple of places and eyeing the edge of my glass. "You should turn yourselves in, you know. Best thing for everyone. You haven't done anything that cannot be forgiven eventually."

"Oh, give me a minute," I said.

"Think of your family, Charlotte," he said sternly.

I suppressed the sudden urge to laugh and moved him closer to the panel. "Think of your *Ark*, Charles."

An appeared quickly, as though she'd been standing in a

control room. She was a bright, clear-cut holo on the shield nearest us, and I straightened involuntarily. She was imposing even when translucent. "Charles," she said, taking in the scene with calculating eyes. If she drew any conclusions, she revealed nothing. "Everests."

In response, I moved Charles front and center.

"Your Imperial Highness," said Charles.

"You've been awfully busy lately," I said, my voice hard, "so I'll keep it short. Adam is here. But I suspect you knew that, even if the EuroArk refuses to believe it." The holo glitched slightly, giving the impression of a blink, but An was immobile, so I continued. "By rights, you should have been my ally. We want exactly the same thing."

"I have allies, Char. I warned them not to be so foolish with you. Others may underestimate you, but I never have."

My hand was cold against the glass. I shifted my grip, shoving my sleeve between my skin and the blade, and returned it to Charles' throat. "Well, I don't have allies," I said. "When you destroyed the Remnant, you destroyed everything."

"We're moving on Adam," said Eren. "Tell Shan to help us."

She laughed, a quick, mirthless grunt. "Release Mr. Eiffel, Char."

"Give me a way to decouple Adam from the life support system on my Ark, and he's all yours," I said.

"It cannot be done," she said. "Any attempt will trigger the failswitch." There was a pause, and her eyes found mine through the holo. "I am sorry."

"Remove Eren's k-band, then."

"I'm afraid I can't do that either," she said. "It's been slaved to Adam for some time now. He left my channel open, but I suspect that even that will be closed soon." I

175

gritted my teeth, trying to figure out my next move, and An spoke again. "It seems we are of no use to each other."

An was never one to respond to weakness, but it wasn't my style anyway. "You're wrong about that," I said. "I intend to end this, one way or another. And I won't let him hurt my Ark, so I suggest you start looking for ways to disable the failswitch. Pretty please. You can look me up when you're ready to play nice."

The steel in her voice cut through the holo. "I'm not playing at all, Char. This was never a game for me." There was a pause, but her voice did not soften. "I regret that it had to end this way."

A sense of dread worked its way through my skull as her meaning set in. "Wait! An. You don't mean that."

Beside me, Eren paled. "Please, An," he began. "It hasn't come to that yet."

"What do you mean?" said Charles.

"She's planning to nuke the Ark," I said quietly.

"Impossible," he said. "She'd never."

"She would. It's the only way to ensure that Adam is dead."

Adam was a threat to her ship, and An would do anything for her ship.

She'd have no qualms about blowing up another Ark.

I was more certain of that than my own name. And when Adam died, so would the North American Ark. She'd kill us all and plant the settlement herself. It was the only way to protect her people.

"We have weapons of our own!" said Charles. "You'll never get away with it."

"I can assure you that mine are still greater, and certainly sufficient for the task. As I said, I do regret it."

176

"An—" Eren began, but her mind was made up.

"Imperial out," she said, executing what might have been a millionth of a bow.

"What about Shan?" I said quietly.

She blinked. "What about him?"

"You'd kill him, too?"

A shadow of hesitation crossed her face as she guessed at my meaning. "I have little patience for hypotheticals, Ms. Turner."

"He's here, An. I saw him."

"He…" An looked at something out of the frame of the holo. "Get Captain Hui on the comm." She turned back to us, eyes narrowed.

"Oh, we'll wait," I said. "A captain, is it? Tell him I said congrats on the promotion."

"He wouldn't leave without my permission," she said.

I raised an eyebrow. "You sure about that?"

The holo blipped as a man's uniform-clad shoulder crossed the scanner. I could tell from his posture that he hadn't brought the Imperial the news she wanted.

An, on the other hand, did not change. Not outwardly, at least. But there was something diminished in her eyes, her speech.

"He doesn't have to die," I told her.

She gave me a dismissive glance. "Such things are beyond you."

"I can save him."

There was a pause as she considered my words. "Exactly what are you suggesting?"

"Give me time. I will take care of Adam myself." My tone had more confidence than my heart.

"I don't believe you. You'd never destroy your own Ark."

"My family is here," I said softly. "An. Don't do it. Give me time to take care of it. There is no risk to you."

"But that is where you are wrong, Charlotte."

"He's threatened them," Charles explained. "There was a time when he thought you might reach out to An, before you came here. But surely—"

"Well, I didn't." I turned to An. "Give us a week."

She laughed coldly. "He contacted me again this morning. An hour."

I smiled. If we were negotiating, I'd already won. She was agreeing to give me a chance in spite of herself. "Think of Shan. Three days."

There was a pause. "Three hours."

That was all I needed to hear. I wasn't going to make it any longer than that, anyway. "Deal. Everest out." I reached for the switch to terminate the feed.

Charles shifted in his seat, ending the brief moment of concentration I'd summoned. "Well, that went well," he said sarcastically.

Eren put a hand on the far side of my waist and gave me a squeeze. When we were halfway to an embrace, he pressed forward, into my shoulder, and blocked Charles from the desk. "Get away from the comms, Mr. Eiffel."

Charles removed his hands, a guarded look on his face.

"What was that? Who were you trying to call?" I asked. "The Council?"

"The gendarmes, actually," said Charles, still maddeningly calm. "It seems our little experiment has run its course."

"Experiment?" Eren frowned.

"She's a tough nut to crack," said Charles. "The usual drugs weren't working. We decided it was better to follow her around for awhile instead. See if we couldn't learn more by observation."

His words sank in slowly. "What are you talking about?" I said.

"When your inevitable escape attempt took place, we sent the bare minimum of soldiers. We *told* them to let you go," Charles said scornfully. "You must think pretty highly of yourself if you thought you could outrun an entire Ark."

"Oh, you'd be surprised," said Eren.

Charles ignored him. "It has proved a fruitful plan. We never dreamed you had allies in the biosphere." He looked at me thoughtfully. "As much as I like you, Ms. Turner, I can't say I'm looking forward to the next step. It will not be pleasant."

"You could have just asked me, you know. No one ever thinks of that." My mind reeled, but I met his eye, suppressing a chill. "Did I give you anything useful?" I asked, angry now. "Any information you might want to act on? Like, I don't know, the imminent destruction of your entire ship?"

"Suffice it to say, you do not disappoint." He gave Eren an appraising glance. "We couldn't wake him up ourselves, so we decided to let you have a crack at it. We didn't count on him being so much trouble, though. He hasn't let his eyes off you since he woke up. I had hoped to follow you a bit longer, but *c'est la vie*."

That explained why Charles had tried to discredit me to Eren. Charles lifted his hands. "But no matter. Now we can question you both. The gendarmes will be here any minute." Instinctively, I took a step to the right, angling myself between Charles and Eren.

"No, they won't," I said, my voice like steel. Back home,

that was the first thing people said to Kingston when they found him rifling through their stuff. Me, they rarely caught. But Kingston was bigger, and slower. And a whole lot scarier. Anyway, it was almost never true. "You haven't called them yet."

"You should surrender, both of you," said Charles.

He still didn't get it. Perhaps the horror of our years under Adam's control had passed like a distant nightmare for the rest of the world. They'd escaped easily and gone on their way. They didn't know what we'd been through. Maybe I was a fool to blame them.

It occurred to me that we were going about this all wrong.

"I can't make them believe me. I can't make them chase Adam," I said evenly. "But I bet they'll chase me." I tossed the glass shard aside. It went dark as it hit the carpet. "He's out there. Either we defeat him, or it's all over anyway. For everyone." It was no great loss to be discovered, I reasoned, fighting the heaviness in my heart. Where I was going, there was no coming back. Adam was one move from checkmate. "Alert the gendarmes. Tell them we'll be in the biosphere. And if you want this Ark to survive, you'll tell them Adam never left, and he'll destroy a lot more than a city next time."

Charles looked at me as though for the first time. "Go in peace, Charlotte Turner."

I nodded.

"You sure you want to let him call the police?" said Eren.

"Yeah," I said. I'd finished hiding a long time ago. "Send them. Send them all."

# Twenty

The woods were cool and dark, and the scent of the pines coursed through me as I caught my breath in the shadows. The wind was picking up. In comparison to the dry, circulated air of the ship, the forest felt almost damp.

Or maybe that was the gathering storm.

We'd be too exposed if we went through the field directly in front of the house, but I wanted to case it before I just ran right in. Unfortunately, I couldn't see anything. No lights were on, and the front door was shut.

"They live in that one," I said to Eren, pointing out their cabin from the cover of leaves around us. I glanced at him. "I'm not going to fall over, you know."

He relaxed his grip on my bad arm long enough to take a good look across the field. "Sorry," he whispered. "I know. I wasn't holding on for your sake."

"Hey, you feeling all right?"

"Just thinking about how this is all gonna play out," he said. I put a hand on his upper arm, and he covered it immediately, giving me a quick squeeze. "So it's West and Mars. Maybe Shan. Anyone else?" he asked.

I looked at him, surprised. "I haven't told you yet? They

have a daughter. Cecelia. And a son, too. They adopted one of the lockies. Maxx."

He looked at me in wonder. "Children."

"Yeah."

We held each other's gaze a moment longer. "Huh," he said finally.

"We should go around back. The woods are closer there. Maybe there's a window."

He nodded and led the way through the trees. We were half-running, half-ducking, and half-holding hands. We made pretty good time, all things considered.

"I see two possibilities," I said. "We run in now and try to warn them. Or we wait until dark."

Eren was studying the house. "Wait. Definitely. Mars would have done that already."

*If she made it this far,* I thought. "I vote running now."

"Why am I not surprised? But no. There's a fair chance he's already in there, waiting for us."

I tasted the air. The last time I'd gone up against Adam, he'd sent lightning clouds to kill us. The feeling of electricity in the wind wasn't there yet, but I knew from experience that could change in a single jolt. "There's also a chance he's not going to attack head-on," I told Eren. "I'm guessing he's got a few tricks up his sleeve." An image of Cecelia and her eight-toothed grin flashed through my mind, and my legs moved all on their own. I slipped out of the wooded cover and toward the house.

Eren made a sound that fell somewhere between a choke and a shout. "Hey," he said, stumbling after me. "*Char.*"

"*What?*" I said, running a hand along the back of the cabin. I peered into the window. The lights were out, and I didn't see anyone. I decided to move toward the door.

"*Char. Stop.*" Eren followed behind me, looking panicked.

"Maybe make a little more noise," I hissed. "I'm not sure the gendarmes got a lock on our position yet."

I inched the door open to the exact width of my body and slinked inside, staying in the shadows.

Which wasn't all that difficult, since the lights were out.

Eren, on the other hand, threw open the door and covered me simultaneously, which blocked my view of the room. I gave him an exasperated sigh. Apparently satisfied, he worked his way methodically through the cabin, clearing the space behind the door, underneath the bed, and in the bathrooms.

"You happy now?" I said.

Then he turned to me. "Charlotte," he said, eyes flashing. "You can*not* just run off like that."

I bristled. "*Run off?* What am I, five? We're in the middle of a fight, Eren! The gendarmes are on their way any second now."

"You have to listen to me." He held a hand out, as though he were going to hold me by the shoulders. As if he were going to make me listen.

I jerked back as hard as I could. Flames lit my face, my eyes. "*Don't touch me.*"

"There are ways of doing this—" he began, taking a step forward, but I couldn't hear him at all anymore.

"No. Don't *touch* me. You think this is the first house I ever cased?"

"Just listen to me!" he said, not quite shouting. "You're not trained for this. You can't just—"

"I was *fine.* I was sweeping the area as I went. Not that you would know that, since you probably think I'm just some kind of delinquent."

He shook his head, and I took in the sharp muscle of his jaw when I said the last word. "We're in this together," he said, bringing himself under control. "You cannot just leave without talking to me, even if you don't—"

"They're my *family*. I had to protect them."

He gritted his teeth, speaking every word deliberately. Softly. "You are my family now, Charlotte."

The shock of the words drained the heat from my tongue. From the room. I was quiet. "And I have to protect *you*," he finished.

I thought of my mother. Right then, in the middle of the cabin. I didn't know why. It was like trying to breathe in a burning room. "You, you—" I struggled for the words, but I'd never been one for declarations of love or valor. I felt lost.

He rubbed a spot on the back of his neck, eyes strained, not quite looking directly at me. "It's the only thing I'm good for anymore. I spent the last five years *dreaming* of you. The real you. A real—" He bit off the word, searching me. "Living out my own worst nightmares, just so I could be near you. To protect you. Because *you were right*. This isn't over. And you were wrong, too, about us being finished. Back when you were in the hospital. Because whatever we were to each other, whatever we meant when we got married, it hasn't changed. Not for me."

He was breathing fast, waiting for me to say something. Maybe there was nothing but a hole where my heart should have been, because all I felt was pain. Pain for Eren. For what we'd both been through. I thought of our "marriage," and how, for a brief moment, I had even longed to be his wife, always knowing that it wasn't real. That it could never work.

"I'm sorry for what you've been through. I wish you'd

184

just let me go. I wish you hadn't suffered. Because I don't know what's left of us," I said finally. "I don't even know what's left of *me*. And none of this matters anyway, if we can't get out of this."

He shook his head and took my hand in his, shifting his mother's ring on my finger. "Of course it matters, Charlotte. It's the only thing that does. If you'd wanted to run, you could have."

My head was light, and his hands were warm against mine. "Well. That is what I'm best at. You know. That and the odd felony."

He didn't return my smile. "When are you going to realize that you're worth saving, too?"

I took a measured breath. There wasn't time for this. We needed to—

"Charlotte. I mean it. Look at me." I tilted my head to his, and our eyes met. "*It was worth it.* All those years. All that time waiting for you to come back. Every moment. *You* were worth it."

I was quiet for a long time. "Then I have to protect you, too."

He nodded at me, his face serious. "We're a team, Charlotte."

"And you're wrong, you know."

He gave me an open look.

"You're good for a lot more than just protecting me."

He rolled his eyes, the shadow of a smile finally touching his expression. "Agree to—"

"No. Eren." Gently—barely touching him at all—I put my hand against his neck, in the same spot he'd been rubbing. "I don't know what's going to happen. I don't know what our lives will be like if we make it through this. But I know that you matter." He looked away, and I used my bad arm to bring his face right back to me. "And I am *not* talking about the things your dad wanted for you."

He shifted, suddenly uncomfortable. On an impulse, I kissed him.

He leaned in, taking my head in both his hands, and kissed me back. His fingers were tangled in my hair, and his breath was hot on my neck.

And then he pulled away.

"I missed you," he said, not quite smiling yet.

"I mean, I could think of some other uses for you *right now*. I'm just saying."

At this, he laughed, and the pain ebbed, still rolling, like the lowest tide of the ocean.

The battle began at dusk.

Eren led me back to the trees, where we concealed ourselves once again. I lay on my stomach, closer to him than necessary, wondering what form the attacks would take. I expected lightning. What we got was worse. I focused on the cabin until my body was motionless and my nerves were made of iron.

As if on cue, the air grew cold, and the empty house was silent.

It started with a low rumble that worked its way through the ground beneath my belly. I searched the sky for the killer clouds but saw none. "Earthquake?" Eren mouthed.

I gave him a perplexed shrug.

As I watched, the earth beneath my hands shifted, and I moved my focus to the grains of dirt between my fingers. They lifted up into the air, then dropped. I felt the fall in my belly.

Gasping, I grabbed Eren by the arm. He'd felt it, too. "It's the grav generator," he said into my ear. "That's gotta be Adam."

I nodded grimly. There was only one reason he'd haunt the biosphere instead of the rest of the ship. Me.

I put my bad arm over his in the gathering darkness. "We have no weapons," I said. "No access to the controls. This is a deathtrap." I took a breath. He could still surrender, get amnesty. "Because—this is it for me, Eren. I'm not leaving until it's done."

He held my gaze until we understood each other, then stacked his other hand on top of my arm. He wasn't leaving, either.

In the distance, a twig snapped. "They're coming," said Eren.

"They're here," I murmured back.

Behind us, a branch rustled and revealed a soldier. There was no other word for it. He wore fatigues and carried a military-grade assault rifle. He wasn't much taller than I was, and he was probably younger. He advanced through the trees with the confidence of youth and training and was followed by four other soldiers at staggered intervals, taking cover behind the trees.

When they were barely past, another twig snapped, much louder this time.

No, not a twig. There was a light buzzing noise, followed by a second crack, and the young man fell to the ground. His face hit the dirt at the same time as the rest of him. He shuddered and stopped moving.

The battlefield burst into action. I heard a buzz, like being near a hive of bees, off and on, and it took a moment before I realized there were bullets overhead. I hit the ground, pressing my cheek into the dirt, and beside me, Eren was doing the same.

I heard a man shout out behind me and switched to face the other way, trying to cover my head with my hands, still pressing the side of my face into the dirt. I couldn't see the first shooter.

"Are they shooting at each other? Why?" I said, my voice pitched high.

"Separate troops," Eren said, no longer whispering. "I don't think the gendarmes expected opposition."

"Well, I know I didn't."

"Your father?" he asked.

"No. Not a chance." This was far from his style. I knew too well that he'd prefer to let me get arrested peacefully, then fight it out in court later, if at all. He certainly wouldn't want to kill anyone.

"Who, then? An couldn't have landed an army here," he said. "They'd have seen her."

The bullets intensified, and I squirmed my way back toward a tree like an animal, never letting my belly off the ground. I heard more screams from deep in the woods.

My instinct was to grab the fallen soldier's rifle, but Eren grabbed my wrist. "No, Char. Stay down." I looked back at the rear of the cabin and tried to decide whether its walls were thick enough to block the fire. Not that it mattered. I'd be dead if I stood. I peered through the space between the cabins to the field on the other side. It wasn't long before the grass moved, and I saw the face of another soldier in the field on the other side. He was not alone.

"Look, they're in the field!"

Eren squinted through the cabins. "Not our problem," he said softly. "Your family's not in there."

At that moment, the grass exploded. A strong whistle filled the air, and I felt Eren's arms squeezing my back and shoulders. His right hand covered my head, pressing me harder into the dirt. Another explosion, but this time, all I could hear was a high-pitched whine.

Eren slid backwards and pulled my leg. I met his eye, and he mouthed something.

"What?" I screamed.

He mouthed the same word again, and I realized I couldn't hear anything anymore: not the blasts, not the buzz of bullets. I shook my head, gluing my body in place. I didn't want to move. I couldn't.

He pulled harder, more insistently, mouthing the same word over and over.

I wanted to scream.

He grabbed the other leg, shifting himself half-upright, and I came to my senses for a brief moment. Eren had to stay down. If I had to back up to keep him on the ground, I would. "No!" I shouted. "I'm coming!"

We slithered back with surprising speed. When we were well past the dead soldier, Eren stood to a crouch. "Get back down!" I said.

"We have to get away from here. We need to—"

He pulled me up until my feet hit the ground, and I began to run as though carried by wings. Trees flew past. The occasional branch whipped across my face, but I felt nothing, thanks to my fear-laced adrenaline. A vague part of my brain wanted me to calm down, to think, but all I could do was run. I felt my fear slip down into panic with every thumping step. We were approaching the edge of the biome, and then what would we do?

"We need better cover!" I screamed. "A bigger tree!"

Laura Liddell Nolen

Eren was shaking his head. His hand covered my mouth, and he dragged me into a clump of trees. "Whisper, Char. Just breathe. There aren't bigger trees. They're all the same age," he said, and I realized that I could hear him. "Artillery," he murmured, thinking. He focused on the sky, the horizon, the other trees, then moved his hand to my forehead, trying to calm me. "Shouldn't be possible." He dragged a sleeve over his face, knocking some of the dirt off onto the back of my neck, and I realized that he must have been afraid, too. "Why are they fighting? Why are they *armed*?"

"I think they always were," I said, trying desperately to slow my breathing. My mind, on the other hand, had the opposite problem. I needed to wake it up, but it was like my head was full of cotton. I was unprepared for any of this. "I think they had weapons from the beginning."

"No, think about it. They couldn't have," he said, his voice husky. "Don't you see? Those were artillery shells. Someone is prepared to fight a battle."

I shook my head, straining to catch my breath.

"A *land* battle. Who could have predicted that? Someone who planned to invade ahead of time." He shut his eyes. "Way ahead of time."

"Not necessarily," I wheezed. "Could just be someone with a knack for killing and few weeks of spare time. Anyone come to mind?"

"*Hey*," came a voice. We froze in each other's arms, and I felt the thump of Eren's heart against my back..

"Char. Eren."

We looked around, perplexed. "Mars?" I whisper-shouted.

The bushes parted, and Mars slipped in. She was truly a sight. Twigs and leaves adorned most of her back and chest,

190

and her face was covered in dark brown mud. Eren and I made room for her.

"How did you find us?" I said. "Where are the kids? Where is West?"

"I've been following you since you got here." She shook her head, glancing at Eren's metallic k-band. "And no idea. Everything seemed fine when I got here, except that they were gone. So I left an alert and hid. With any luck, West will have seen it." She let out a breath full of tension. "He'll have seen it and taken my babies far away from this place."

"What kind of alert?" said Eren.

"I left the broom on the back porch. Something we worked out when we got here, in case we were caught."

"That's pretty smart," I said.

"You don't have to sound so surprised," she said. "Thieves do it."

"I mean, I just used a walkie-talkie," I shrugged. "Less room for interpretation. But you think West saw it? Or is there a chance he missed it?"

"Those are the options," Mars said archly.

I grunted. "Sure. Or they could have been arrested before they got there. They could be hiding. They could have been arrested *after* they got there."

"If they'd been arrested, someone would have been waiting for us, too," Eren pointed out.

"Wait a minute," I said. "Where was the broom? The front porch or the back?"

"Back," she said. "Why?"

"Because," I said, feeling slightly dizzy, "there is no broom on the back porch."

She held my gaze for an instant, then dismissed the thought. "You just didn't see it."

191

"Mars," I said, my voice low. "I can remember what things look like. *Exactly* what they look like. I can picture the porch as we walked in. There was no broom."

Her small face went pale. "You're wrong. I put the broom there."

"Then you've had a visitor," I said darkly.

Mars took another second to process that and prepared to leave. Eren caught her by the arm. That was a mistake. "If you are fond of that hand, I suggest you let go," she hissed, all anger now.

But Eren did not flinch. "We need to think about this," he said quietly.

"I'm pretty sure 'visitor' is the correct response," she said, reaching for her gun. "This is a battle zone, Everest," she continued, her voice full of ice. "And my children are out there. So let. Go."

Eren's other arm loosened around my chest as he made a point of straightening. "I know we've had our differences, Marcela." I twisted in his lap to give him a quizzical look. I'd never considered the possibility that Mars could dislike anyone more than me, but based on the look on her face and the fact that he still hadn't released her, Eren was making a fairly successful run at the position. "I was perhaps not her favorite prisoner," he explained, referring to his brief stint as a prisoner of war in the Remnant. "But I pledge to you that I will help you find them. Now sit back down. We have to be smart about this."

The gun came down, not quite in line with his face. Which was why I didn't jump her right then. "You're gonna want to put that gun down, Mars," I said quietly.

"He's still a Guardian to me. His pledge is worth nothing."

"Well, only one of us has worked up close with Adam

for the last half a decade and can remember a solid minute of it, and it wasn't you or me," I said. "So here's *my* pledge: sit down so we can work through this together, and I will protect your children with my life." She gave me a long look, and I saw that she knew I meant it. "West, too."

She gave a terse nod and sheathed the gun. "Let's hope it doesn't come to that," she said, looking like she might run at any moment.

Eren cleared his throat. "First, we should just say it: Adam took the broom."

"We don't know that," said Mars. He gave her a sympathetic look.

"We have to assume that it's a signal to us," I cut in. "To me."

"I agree," he said. "He wants us back at the cabin."

I shivered, and his arms tightened around me. "Even if we wanted to walk right into his trap, we can't hope to get there alive," I said. "The fields are full of soldiers. We're still in the middle of a battle."

"Speaking of soldiers, that's not really Adam's style, is it?" said Mars. "He always hated that part. He's more cloak and dagger."

The chill deepened its grip on my chest. "Yeah," I agreed, pulling Eren even closer. "I think we can agree that he's just getting started."

"So, what'll it be this time? Lightning?" she asked. "Drugs?"

I shook my head slowly. "I'm thinking he's graduated from that."

"We can't plan for something we can't predict," Mars snapped.

"Microgravity?" I said. "Did you feel a thump earlier? Or, you know. Whatever the opposite of a thump is."

"Yeah, I feel them," she said.

"They're three minutes apart," said Eren.

"What? More than once?" I looked from one face to the other.

Mars raised her eyebrows. "Yeah. Way more than once. Put your hand on the ground. We're due another."

Cautiously, I placed a hand in the dirt, dreading what I already knew I'd feel. Sure enough, the *thump* landed a few moments later, jarring the earth around my knuckles. My heart rate picked up. I think I'd been feeling it all along, but my mind hadn't wanted to deal with it. But the thump was there. And it was getting stronger.

"Any bright ideas about how to—" Mars began, but a quiet *snap* interrupted her.

A moment brushed past in strained silence, and I looked at Mars, at a loss.

But instead of Adam's voice, or another soldier, I heard a burbling hoot and the rustling of feathers.

A flock of swans bustled their way into the clearing, waddling hard, like they were late to a meeting. One brushed into my leg, and I shifted to move out of its path. It was tall enough to make me nervous, had I not been occupied by more pressing matters. I'd never seen a swan up close.

In spite of its size, its neck was so long that I couldn't help but think it delicate. Breakable. As I moved out of its way, it twisted up to fix me with a curious expression, then hurried after its family. A second later, another *crack* broke through the trees, and the first swan took flight.

Suddenly, they flew. All around us, the giant birds winged

their way up through the trees. It was a flurry of urgent honks and scuffling, bristled feathers.

The moment and the swans passed us by.

And then the wind began to blow, whipping my hair into my face. The trees bent, gently at first, but then hard, like toughened rubber, until they were unable to withstand the strength of the growing gale. When the one before me broke in half at the base, it made an enormous *CRACK* that echoed through the forest.

And then the dirt was flying. Mars and Eren looked worried.

My heart sank as I took in their faces. I'd have saved them all, if I'd had the strength to stop him. Given the chance, I'd have traded my life for the ship. But I was swept up in Adam's game along with everybody else.

"Run!" Eren shouted. "Run for the door!"

I shook my head, picturing the scene from Adam's point of view. No one was getting out of here. What would be the fun in that?

Now the wind was preternaturally strong. Together, we scrambled for purchase against the onslaught. If we weren't completely helpless yet, we soon would be.

I heard a sound like a train and searched the sky, finally able to guess what Adam had in store for us. In the distance, the air split in half and roiled into a deadly, twisting rope. Mars stood and scrambled for a tree. I brushed against her back with my good arm, taking her gun and shoving her toward the nearest, strongest one I could find while throwing a final glance at Eren. His eyes were on the sky, and as I watched, the confusion melted into understanding. I shoved Mars' gun down the front of my pants and adjusted it until I was sure it was secure. No way was Adam going to let her near him.

I was the one he was after.

"It's a—" Eren shouted, pulling me toward a tree by my bad arm. I wrapped myself around it, and he wrapped himself around me. It was small, too small for both of us. The pines were five years old, barely stronger than saplings. We'd survive longer if we clung to different trees.

Besides, I had to get away from him. I couldn't think while he was near me. I couldn't afford to have something left to lose, and Eren made everything precious.

"NO! STAY HERE!" I shouted, pressing his hand into the bark. "We have to split up!"

The force grew stronger, and I wanted to scream. It didn't matter, though. No one would hear me if I did. I found a tree of my own and wrapped myself around its base with my legs. The cyclone loomed closer. It took Eren a moment to decide that he'd rather ride out whatever was coming with me, but by then, it was too late. The force of the wind was against him.

Another thump of micrograv, and my brother's beloved biosphere churned into rubble. Nearby, Mars wrapped herself around a tree. Too late, I realized that that didn't matter, either.

At last, I understood. *He's not going to stop.* That was the game. "*He's going to kill us!*"

Gravity gave way in pieces. My feet left the dirt, and I heard a sound like a wild gurgle escape from deep inside my belly. I was screaming now. I wrapped my legs around the tree, and to my horror, I felt its roots loosen beneath my thighs.

Debris stung my arms, my face. Larger and larger chunks of flora streamed past. I couldn't dodge them all. I was losing visibility by the second.

I struggled to regain composure, but what was the point? *He's never going to stop until we're dead.*

My hips left the ground. One more thump of zero-grav and the tree to which I clung would become part of the twister, and me with it. It was pointless to hang on. I knew, deep in my soul, that the tornado would not stop while there was life in the biosphere. It twisted, dancing, killing everything it touched.

And it was getting closer.

I looked back at Eren. Maybe there was time to say goodbye.

A flash of silver rocketed into the ether, and I realized that Eren had ripped the foil from his wrist. He was screaming into the k-band.

The tornado twisted closer. My chest left the ground. This was no natural thing. But then, I thought, neither was anything in the biosphere. It was nearly over now. This Ark would fall to Adam.

I suppressed a wild giggle. As soon as that happened, An would blow it up.

She wouldn't even hesitate.

One final look at Eren. The twister jerked nearer, moving like a child with a hula hoop. I prepared to kick myself into his arms. One final embrace.

I gritted my teeth and let go of the tree. My body flew through the air toward Eren, and he caught me. I wrapped myself around him with everything I had. Adam must have loosened the gravity again, because the air was full of dirt. It was getting harder to breathe.

Was there anything he couldn't control? Anything out of his reach?

Eren was shouting again, but all I heard was the twister,

and death. When it picked up speed again, we wouldn't last a moment.

And then it hit me. There was one thing Adam couldn't control.

The reason he was here.

Me.

I brought Eren's wrist to my mouth and screamed for all I was worth. I didn't think he could hear me, but the game was ending, and I had one final card to play.

"I surrender! I SURRENDER!" I took a breath through my sleeve, gasping, but it was a poor filter. The earth was all around. A tree flew past, and as its branches slammed into the other trees, they fell.

I thought of the swans. The curious one. He'd surely died by now.

And then my tree broke free of the ground. Dirt filled the air, and I could no longer see. A weight slammed into my shoulder, but Eren bore the brunt of its impact. He was still clinging to me, protecting me. I prepared to scream again, but a second blow took my breath away. A sharp, massive object crashed into my thigh, sending bright, white flashes of unbearable pain directly through my skull.

*"I surrender. I give up! Adam, PLEASE!"*

We were falling and falling and falling and nowhere was down. Another tree flew past. The next one could kill us. I coughed violently, unable to draw a clean breath, and choked the words at the k-band:

*"You win, Adam. You win."*

And it stopped.

The earth hit the ground.

The ground *existed*, and we lay upon it, buried in dirt up to our waists.

Mars was long gone. Eren had a gash across the back of his neck, and blood spilled forward and over his chest as he covered me.

I realized he'd been screaming, too. His face was white, and I saw that the blood was over my arms and back.

It was so much blood.

If he were ever going to have a chance, I could not waver. I could not stop.

The k-band popped twice, and I thought I heard laughter.

"Very well, Char," came the voice. "I accept."

# Twenty-one

My right thigh was too badly injured to support my weight, and I made my way to the cabin on my hands and knees. It was a poor penance. If I shot Adam, it would kill every soul on board the North American Ark.

If I didn't kill him, he'd never stop. Not ever.

Perhaps I should shoot myself.

The biosphere was razed to the ground. All around, there was nothing but flat, brown destruction. Loose soil and clumps that used to be trees. Nothing moved, and everything was the same color as the dirt. There were no fields, no forests.

The cabin was untouched.

I entered slowly, still crawling. Even though I knew he was there, the sight of him nearly killed me. He was flanked by soldiers. His face was smug but serious, and not a single strand of his hair was out of place.

We faced each other in the small room, Adam and I, surrounded by freeze-framed chaos. The shards of my brother's life were all around. Although the tornado hadn't affected his home, the lack of gravity had come close to total destruction.

We did not speak.

Moving slowly, never letting my eyes off him, I crawled across the floor to an overturned chair, and bracing myself against the floor with my bad arm, righted it. It took awhile. Every limb weighed a thousand pounds.

Adam waited patiently as I climbed into the chair and slumped into a sitting position. The look on his face made my blood cold.

I was so tired.

"Check her." Adam waved at a soldier, who loomed toward me. I held up my hand.

"Stay away from me."

The soldier did not stop, and I realized that he'd been drugged. Of course, I thought thickly. They all were. How else could he have come up with an army capable of standing off against the EuroArk's forces?

"Now, what kind of surrender is that?" Adam asked, a dangerous edge to his voice. "I just want to make sure you're not dying. Yet."

I wet my lips. I really was so tired. Only a little longer, and sleep would envelop me. "Your concern is touching. This isn't my blood." I rolled my sleeve and offered up my veins. "Let's get this over with."

"Oh, Char. I don't need to drug you any more. I don't even care if you have a weapon. We're beyond that now." He laughed, throwing his head back, and I saw my chance.

"Good," I grunted. "Decouple life support and I'm all yours."

Adam laughed again, a loud, hollow sound. "I'm afraid I can't do that." Although his body was grown, he sounded very much like a child. The tight, freezing wad in my throat grew larger, and I swallowed against it. There was no need to be brave anymore, was there? I would die. Others would live. It was a good trade.

My life was never meant to be so precious.

I did not want to listen to the fear that seeped into every pore in my body, but couldn't help wondering how he'd do it. Would it be a bullet? Gas?

No, he'd have something special for me. I thought of the void surrounding the ship, of the airlocks, and shivered. I would never be warm again, but it didn't matter now.

Adam offered no clues, and although I'd resigned myself to my fate, I wasn't exactly eager to die right away. Especially not like that—gasping for air, turned inside-out by the vacuum.

Ninety seconds. More for a person.

"Bring him in!" Adam stepped to the side, and the rear door swung open. One soldier entered, and then another. Then my face went hot, and I felt myself begin to whimper. Eren was stretched between them. He was a bloody, dirty mass with blond hair, and when his shoulder twitched against their grip, I heard myself crying. Adam laughed yet again. "Now that, you probably expected. After all, I can track him anywhere in the universe." He came closer. "And just so we never get complacent, I went ahead and took out an extra insurance policy."

"Adam," I sobbed, "please." He ignored me.

"Joe! Show her what's behind door number two!" Adam commanded. "I have no idea what his name is. He just looks like a Joe, you know?"

Another soldier opened the back door. Horror curled its bony fingers around my heart and began to squeeze. I gasped for air, but nothing helped.

There, between two men, was West.

He was pale, listless, and I thought for a moment that he'd been beaten, but a closer look revealed no apparent injuries. He was gasping, deep in the throes of the Lightness.

"Now, you'll never believe this," said Adam, "but this guy came running back in here right before I set off a tornado!" He gave me a big smile, and I felt sick. "You liked that, didn't you, Char. Anyway, I thought I'd let him see it firsthand, since he was so eager."

"You don't have to do this," I said, my voice strangling. "Just let them go."

"Oh, Char. You still haven't worked it all out, have you? I am never letting them go. Just like I'm never drugging you again. It'll be the real Char all the time. Or I'll kill them."

"An. An knows you're here. She'll blow it all up."

"Oh, she will, will she? Other Joe!" Adam sang out. "Show her door number three!"

I looked on, speechless, as the soldier opened the door. Shan entered the room. His face was badly bruised, and there was blood around his nose. "Adam," I breathed.

"I know, right? It's an exciting day. Just like that, I win!"

"You can't win, Adam," Shan said, his voice deep and sure in spite of his situation. "She will stop you."

A nod from Adam, and Other Joe delivered a blow to Shan's gut so hard I held my breath until I heard Shan suck in again. "You are aware that I have an *army*, yes?" Adam crowed. "And let me see, what else? Right. *You.* She won't harm this ship in a million years. I've read every transmission you sent her."

"You don't know her at all," he croaked.

Adam gave him a cold glance. "It would appear that you are mistaken. But just for giggles, let's call her up! No, no, Char. Stay right where you are."

I looked up, frozen, and returned to my chair. I wanted to be with West. I wanted to protect Eren. More than anything else, I wanted to kill Adam. But I couldn't. Not yet.

Adam dropped a disc-like puck into the center of the room, and I recoiled from it instinctively. "It's just a comm, Char," he sneered. "No need to look so scared."

The holo flipped up into the room, bright and pale, and An took in the scene. When she saw Shan, she straightened herself fully upright. She did not speak.

"An! Good to see you!" Adam said. "We were hoping you could settle something for us. See, I told them that you'd never hurt Shan. But Shan here, he thinks you're just gunning to blow us all up anyway."

Adam put a hand on top of Shan's head and grabbed a fistful of hair. "Tell her, Shan."

"Release him," she said, her voice like a blade.

"Fugitives need hostages, right?" said Adam, mocking her. "Now I have one of yours."

Her gaze cut through the room, burning into each of us in turn. "You are unwise to test me."

I gritted my teeth and tried to think of my next move as Adam continued to taunt her. "Looks like your spy has failed," he said in a surprised voice. "Who'd have thought!"

At this, Shan lifted his head, shaking Adam's grip on his hair, and met An's eye. They stayed that way for a long time. When An replied again, her voice was distant, as though she were speaking to someone else. Even when her voice was soft, the words were laced with danger. "I was chosen to rule this Ark when I was nine years old. Did you know that?"

Adam shook his head, all nonchalance, but I was frozen. This was not the tone I'd expected. "An—" I whispered.

"My parents were exalted in our community. My father was so proud, so happy, and so was I. But my mother never smiled when they spoke of it. I could not imagine why. I was only a child, which is to say that I was a fool." Her last sentence seemed pointed at Adam.

"We can still figure this out, An," I said. Adam snorted at that, but An acted like we weren't even there.

"Give him back to me," she said, her expression torn. Hers was not a voice accustomed to begging.

"'Fraid I can't do it, An," said Adam. "We all know what happens next. I am, however, willing to extend my previous offer."

I looked at him, wondering what horrible thing he'd demanded from her.

"I will never surrender my weapons, Adam."

"Then we will never colonize Eirenea. Are you hearing this, Char?"

I looked at him, unsure of what he meant.

"Yeah, that's right!" he said. "They can't engineer a radiation shield." He made a baby voice, mocking her. "They don't have the technology without Ark Five. And Ark Five is never coming back."

I gave Adam a blank look. If he turned back to An, I could pull out my gun and shoot him. Couldn't I?

"You will not live to see Eirenea colonized," An said. "I give you my word that you will die before that."

"Tell Char what I told you! Tell her, An!" Adam said. He grabbed a gun from the nearest puppeted soldier and aimed it at Shan's forehead. "Tell her."

A flash of worry crossed her face, and she spoke. "Adam claims to be able to solve the problem of the atmosphere. He believes me fool enough to give him all my warheads."

"I don't take you for a fool, An, but clearly you needed some convincing." Adam waved the gun around, giddy. "I did solve the problem. What do you think I spent the last five years doing? No offense, Char, but you're not the best company when you're drugged." His voice was the only sound in the room. My fingers inched closer to the gun, and I folded my body down, hiding them. "I can engineer the poles. I can build an atmosphere. *I can terraform Eirenea.* All I need is her nukes. Tell her about the clouds, Char! Tell her about the twister!"

I looked at An. She laughed, but the sound was split with sorrow. I was sure the sorrow was the stronger part. "What my mother knew at once was hidden from me until the meteor struck, and my childishness vanished along with everything else." She paused, frozen, still staring at Shan. He gave her a look of stone. "It is a hard thing to be a queen. It consumes me." Her gray eyes met mine. "I have no other purpose."

For a moment, she sounded like a different person, and I searched her face, wondering why she suddenly set me off-balance, and it hit me that Adam had made a huge mistake.

"Oh, don't sound so sad," Adam continued, oblivious. "I'll give him right back as soon as you make the delivery." I shook my head, my eyes locked on the Imperial. Her head was half-bowed, and she was staring at Shan as though memorizing him. She seemed smaller than before.

Adam didn't know it yet, but the game was over. He'd gambled and lost.

"We can still have peace, An," I said. "Together."

She gave me a sad smile. "Perhaps you are as naïve as my father, all those years ago. I hadn't thought it. Farewell, Captain Hui."

He jerked to the side, biting into the collar of his robe, and turned his face away from the Imperial. "Stop him!" Adam shouted, understanding his mistake at last. He pulled Shan's jaw apart, but we were too late. My fingers found the gun, for all the good it would do me.

Shan began to shake, then watered at the mouth. His drool turned from clear to white, foaming, and he began to choke. Time slowed to a sickening pace, as though we were treading water in a vat of glue. "Oh, oh," said Adam. He looked confused. "Now that's a surprise."

Shan twitched again and was still.

I turned back to An, my mouth open in horror.

If her voice was like steel before, now it was a raging fire. It consumed the air in the room, calling us to its flames. "Cursed be your head, for his death is on it."

"An! Don't do it, An," I said. "Please!"

"The European Ark has enough missiles to defend itself for a little while." She blazed through the holo like a vengeful ghost, and I felt my breath shorten. "But you can't stop them all."

"Give us a chance!" I screamed. "An, please."

Adam stepped on the disc, smashing it, and the holo blipped out. "You, come with me. We're leaving. You," he said to the soldier. "Bring the others. What's left of them. May as well leave that one," he said, pointing at Eren. "He's not long for this world. Of course, neither is anything else on this Ark."

I moved, whimpering, as Adam grabbed my arm. He dragged me through the door of the cabin. From the porch, in the absence of the trees, I could see all the way to the white walls of the biome. "Please, Adam, please," I heard myself saying. "Let them go. I'll stay with you. I'll—"

He stopped suddenly, and shook me by the shoulders so hard my teeth rattled. The gun slipped down a notch, and I pressed my stomach out, trying to trap it against my waistband. "Shut up. Shut *up*," he was saying. "Just—just shut up, Char. I have a backup plan."

He moved faster, dragging me with him, and we reached the edge of the biome. When he shoved me through the door, I drew a breath.

The hall was full of soldiers.

For an instant, I felt a spring of hope, but it didn't last. Halfway down the hall, Adam stopped, and I realized that they were all drugged. "Ta-da!" he said as we rounded a corner. The ones nearest us had Mars by both arms. She was alive, but only just. Her face dripped with blood and dirt. "Door number four. Blah, blah. Meant for that to go differently," Adam muttered. "Keep moving."

I shuffled forward, rubbing the tears from my eyes. I needed to be able to see straight.

"Char, Char, Char," Adam was talking faster now, fairly shoving me down the hall. "You don't need to cry about it. I'm not going to kill them unless you make me."

I hiccupped, feeling the gun shift in my pants. My brother's face floated forward in my mind. I didn't think I could shoot Adam, even though I had no choice. I thought of all those people on my own Ark. I thought of Eren.

I didn't think I could do it.

"Open up!" he shouted. I snapped back to my senses as Adam muscled me through a nondescript door at the end of the hallway. "Leave her; bring him," he called back to a soldier, waving at Mars and West. Mars was pulled away from West and dragged down the hall. There was murder in her eyes. West remained half-curled. He was still making

208

a sound like a slight moaning whine, deep in the grip of the Lightness.

A soldier-puppet took hold of both my arms, securing me into a standing position, and I gathered what wits I could. The room inside was a perfect circle, with a ring of recessed lights. The walls were black and undecorated. The room was mostly occupied by a massive round table placed precisely in its center. It was plain enough to look at, but it buzzed with importance. Power.

I took in the demisphere in the center of the table and the six enormous, yellow, cushioned chairs around it and blinked. This was the control room. We were standing at the seat of Europe's High Council.

The chairs were empty, and I was shoved into the nearest one. As I hit the cushion, I caught the eye of a Council-member. They were bound and gagged and huddled pitifully along one wall. They were also unguarded, so they must have been drugged as well.

West was flung through the door beside me. He hit the table, then recoiled pitifully. A puppet grabbed him and forced him to stand. My anger flared, but I couldn't afford to lose my temper just yet. I breathed out through my nose. Seeing me, Adam smiled.

"So," he said, flinging himself into a chair, hands behind his head. "Where are the kids?"

At this, West raised his head. The moaning stopped.

"Yeah, I know about them," said Adam. "I'll make you a deal. Tell me where they are, and I'll let you bring them with us."

"No!" I began, but the puppet holding me up wrenched my arms painfully, cutting me off.

Seeing me wince, Adam frowned. "Careful, Joe." He gave

209

an exasperated sigh and turned back to West. "An's going to blow this Ark to smithereens," he said menacingly, putting special emphasis on the last word, "and I am offering you the chance to save your children."

The blank fear drained from my brother's face, and he met Adam's eye with a look that would level a tractor. "You will never have my children," he said simply.

Adam stood. "Is that so?" He produced a stick and held it to West's face. "We'll see about that."

The stick ignited, sending a jolt through West, whose involuntary scream filled the room. I shrieked, but a gloved hand covered my mouth immediately, silencing me.

The screaming stopped, and Adam stood over my brother's body. A cold laugh filled the room, and I held my breath.

But the laugh didn't belong to Adam. West pushed himself to a sitting position and grabbed the stunner, holding it to his own neck. "Come on, Adam. I'd always heard you were smarter than that."

Adam took in my brother's face, bruised and bleeding, and stepped back. "Fine," he said, returning the stunner to his jacket. "Suit yourself." He flopped back into the chair and produced the long, thin wand from his sleeve. "Joe," he called. "Where are we on prep?"

"Nearly there, sir—" Joe began. The door behind him sucked open. Adam tensed, then relaxed as Charles Eiffel entered the room, escorted by yet another soldier-puppet. I frowned. Charles was moving as though underwater, his face perfectly blank. He sure didn't seem like he needed an escort.

"Just the man I need to see!" Adam said. "Mr. Eiffel, I'm having some trouble with your control panel. I wonder if you'd be willing to assist me in breaking in?"

Charles stepped forward and placed a hand on the mound in the center of the round table. He gazed at it as it glowed yellow around his hand, allowing it to scan his retinas.

"And, pulse scan—and we're in!" said Adam. "Have a seat, will you?" Charles sat. "Now that you're here," Adam continued, "you might as well make yourself useful. How many missiles are we down?"

A few taps later, and Charles spoke. His voice was monotone, and he looked straight ahead. "None."

Adam frowned. "And how many has she fired?"

"None."

"No one has fired? At all?" He gave a frustrated grunt. "Show me."

Charles leaned back, giving Adam plenty of space to see the display on the surface of the table in front of his chair.

"Ah. She lacks the nerve. I can fix that. The launch codes, Mr. Eiffel."

"Charles!" I said, realizing what Adam was about to do. "Wake up!"

"It's no use, Char," Adam said. He gave a little snicker. "No one's immune but me. You should hear yourself. If anyone knows it's no use, it should be you."

"First key: K-two-eight-nine-H," said Charles, utterly without inflection. "Second—"

"Somebody should really be writing this down," said Adam. "Joe. Get over here."

Adam pushed back the puppet's sleeve and pulled out a pocketknife. Joe flinched slightly as the blade cut into his forearm. "Nine, H," Adam said slowly. "Hold *still*, Joe. Honestly. Please continue, Mr. Eiffel."

"Second key: B-six-four-Q," Charles droned. Adam completed his carving in Joe's arm, making a show of sticking

211

out his tongue to focus on his work, and dabbed away the blood with his sleeve. Joe looked pale, but he did not react. I felt nauseated.

"Well, that should do it," Adam said. "You stay close to me."

There was a knock on the door, and another puppet entered. "Your jet is ready, sir," said the soldier.

Adam looked at me brightly. "That's our cue!" He pulled his wand in tight and pressed a few buttons on the panel in front of Charles, then looked at the ceiling expectantly.

A burst of water broke through an overhead pipe, then another.

And then the control room was flooding.

"Now, don't worry about that. It's just that I hacked into the water main and gave it my special treatment. Let me just sync the controls to my screen, launch the first strike, and we can get moving!"

"Adam, please—"

"Ugh, do you ever get tired of *saying* that? Don't worry. You're safe. Even West is safe, as long as you cooperate. The two of you will never be separated again. That's what you wanted, right? I have a plan, Char. To the jet!" he said. "Let's show that Lieutenant what she's missing, shall we?"

He shoved me forward, and the blue hallway was streaming with water. As we stepped out into the flood, the speakers crackled to life around us.

"ATTENTION, ALL PERSONNEL, YOU ARE INSTRUCTED TO AVOID THE WATER. STAY IN YOUR HOMES AND TAKE COVER. THE MILITARY IS WORKING TO NEUTRALIZE THE THREAT."

He shoved me down the hall. I focused on the bright yellow rings on the floor beneath me, trying to keep my balance. West was pressing forward, angling against his captors to get closer to me. The message repeated itself. "ATTENTION, ALL PERSONNEL—"

Adam laughed. "Yeah, good luck with that." We turned a corner, and Adam stopped short, holding out a hand. West drew in a breath. I suppressed a cheer.

There, in the center of the corridor, was Mars, but she was no longer restrained. She was flanked by armed soldiers, and their weapons were aimed at Adam.

"Oh, I don't think we need the luck," she said.

Adam paused for a brief moment, then tightened his grip on my arm. A puck hit the floor. Its effects were immediate: a flash of lightning, accompanied by a jolt straight through the hallway. I screamed, feeling like I'd been hit by a stunner, and Adam laughed again. The smoke had a familiar taste, and it occurred to me that it was probably laced with his drug. The blue walls ran white with rushing water, and the smoke concealed everything else. "You people have no idea what you're fighting for," he said. "I'm the only one who can save you. But I guess that doesn't make a difference right now. Attack!" He threw another puck, and it fizzed and began to smoke, obscuring the fight.

Adam pulled me down a new hallway and deeper into his army, hurling me over the micrograv spaces and flipping me onto my side as the change in gravity caught me. Walls became floors, and smoke was everywhere. Water poured down all around us, gathering forcefully into churning spheres in the places without gravity.

I made a fist and jerked away from his grip. "You can't fight it, Char," Adam said, as though annoyed. "The water is drugged. The smoke is drugged. Knock it off."

I tripped, trying to watch the scene behind us through

the smoke as he dragged me along. My brain wanted to pull away. Mars was running through the crowd, shoving a needle into the thigh of every soldier she could get to. Her aim was precise, like a rattlesnake. The soldiers fell, recovering from the drugs. She was magnificent.

"Aah," Adam muttered to himself. "Don't let it scare you. We're gonna have to stop that." He reached into his jacket, and I lunged at him.

I was too late. He threw the puck around a corner, and it changed direction with the gravity. The puck hit Mars square in the chest and began to fizz. Her face went blank, and she fell.

The walls of the hall were an avalanche of rain, and she collapsed onto the floor between them. A pool of water splashed out from around her head as she hit the ground, framing the delicate swirls of smoke that stretched out from the hole in her chest.

"NO!" I screamed. "*NO!*"

I lunged for her, but Adam caught me. "It's too late for her, Char. Keep moving, or your brother's next."

I kept right on screaming, and heavy hands grabbed me, dragging me with Adam. The smell of the drug was all around.

"They can't catch me," Adam was saying. "I have more men than they can count."

I looked at him, eyes wide, barely able to think.

"Yeah," he said. "And An will fire any second now, if she hasn't already. Believe me, we cannot hold her for long."

He took hold of my arm and pulled me along like a doll. I pressed my lips together and wiped the rain from my face with my bad arm. He had to let go of my good arm at some point. Was I strong enough to shoot him?

214

Was strong the right word, anyway?

I thought of Mars.

I thought of Maxx and Cecelia.

I had to kill him. I had to.

After a lifetime of running, we reached our destination: a hangar at the end of a spike. Soldiers lined the halls, standing at attention as we approached the door. They dripped with poisoned water. My pulse quickened. For some reason, the water wasn't affecting me. It had to be me. I had to kill Adam.

"Now, you're gonna like this, Char. I got the best jet ever. Way better than a hopper. It holds more than one passenger, but it retains all the maneuverability of a hopper. And it's armed. Obviously."

The door sucked open, revealing a small private hangar. It was completely black, with a suspended catwalk that extended straight to the outer seal.

It was also completely empty.

Adam turned around slowly.

"Where is my jet?" he asked. I felt myself swallow. He was like a nightmare I couldn't stop dreaming. He was a monster, uncontrollable and unpredictable.

And he was angry. At last, he released my arm and put his face directly into the face of the nearest soldier. "*Where*," he repeated dangerously, "is my *jet*?" The soldier stared at him blankly. "Get me Charles!" Adam shrieked.

Charles was dragged to the front lines, and Adam thrust a screen in his hands. "How many has she fired?" he shouted.

Charles glanced down at the screen. "None, sir," he said quietly.

"Let's see how she feels about this," Adam said. He grabbed Joe's arm and, reading the bloody code carved in skin, launched another missile. Halfway through the process, he looked up, suddenly understanding, and grabbed his wand.

The soldier smiled.

"You're not drugged," Adam said softly.

The soldier shook his head.

"Neither are you," he said to Charles.

Charles shook his head. "I'm afraid not," he replied.

Adam pointed the wand at his face. "The codes, Mr. Eiffel, or you die. The real ones."

I pulled my gun. It was hard and heavy in my hands.

Adam shoved me out of the hangar and back into the corridor, taking in my gun at the same time.

"Bad idea, Char. I'm wired to, like, *everything*," he muttered, not even trying to take it from me. "You wouldn't dare."

The water might not be drugged, but the smoke sure was. It was behind us for the moment, but it drifted forward fast. The sounds of the battle drew closer. "Let's go. Plan B. Or C. I lost track." He paused to find my eyes. "You're not gonna like Plan C. And can SOMEBODY please find my *jet*!"

"The jet is gone, Adam. It's the end of the line."

Adam's puppet soldiers parted, and at the end of the hall stood my oldest friend. He was calm and tall and surrounded by fighters.

And he was armed.

"Isaiah," said Adam. "You know, you're just in time."

# Twenty-two

The moments crowded together in a blur of smoke and pain. Adam reached for me. I aimed the gun at his leg and pulled the trigger. It made a massive *bang* that shook my ribs and broke my thoughts apart like rubble.

Adam cried out in pain and threw me to the ground.

I never hit the ground. Instead, the soldier behind me caught me and wrapped an arm around my neck from behind. The smoke in the hallway was thick enough to taste, and he was well under its influence. I shook my head, trying to clear it.

Limping, Adam leaned down to pick up the gun as though he'd dropped a quarter. "Oh, Char," he said casually. "That was *such* a mistake."

He pointed the gun at my head and looked back at Isaiah. "Pretty sure this is checkmate, right, mate?"

"Don't you stop, Isaiah," I screamed, choking. "Not for me. You kill him. You keep going or I'll never forgive you."

Isaiah stepped forward. "They shoot to kill, Adam," he said carefully. "And if they don't get you, An will. I know you don't want Char to die. Give up. They won't kill you

217

if you surrender. They'll give you to An to force a truce, but they won't kill you."

"Adam," I began.

A crease of worry flashed across Adam's face, but he straightened his back and tightened his grip on the gun. "Shut up. Just shut up. I'm trying to think," he said.

"Nothing left to think about, my friend," Isaiah said. "You can't get out of this."

Adam gritted his teeth and pressed the barrel of the gun into my temple. "I still have a few tricks up my sleeve."

"So do I," Isaiah said.

As I watched, the puppets in the hallway turned as one. Their weapons were drawn in unison.

But instead of pointing at Isaiah, they turned on Adam.

"I recently received a special advisement from a member of the Tribune," Charles said. "It seems he's been working with a refugee who poses as a doctor on our sick bay. We've made some key adjustments to the water supply. I hope you don't mind."

"They're not puppets, Adam. They're free," said Isaiah. "It's over."

Adam glanced at their guns, and for an instant, he looked scared. His eyes went wide, like a little kid. Then he caught himself and gave me a little sigh. "Huh. It certainly is."

He pointed his gun, but not at me.

At West.

"Shoot!" I screamed. "Shoot him!"

But nobody did. They were free men, after all. And they chose to save the North American Ark.

"Now we're even," Adam said to me. He took in my face, my posture. Saw me kick and scream. The soldier behind me had breathed the smoke and was puppeted to Adam. His grip on me was like a steel trap.

Adam smiled.

I felt my heart detach from my body. It drifted up into the shattered air around my brother and continued into the void, that persistent nothingness that had surrounded us since we left Earth, that had tested our will to survive at every moment. For me, the test was finally over.

My heart drifted up toward death.

Adam pulled the trigger.

West fell.

And my heart exploded in the vacuum.

# Twenty-three

I longed for the relentless embrace of space. It called me.

All around me was chaos and fighting. Adam, Isaiah, and so many soldiers.

And my brother, my brother. But the deep groanings of my soul remained unvoiced. I found that I could not breathe, let alone scream, let alone moan with the pain that pulled me out, out of my body and into the stars.

Adam was dragging me toward the hangar when his gun left my temple.

He aimed it at his own head. I heard him shouting as though through an echoing tunnel. He threatened to shoot again; they backed off. For the moment, we were alone in the hallway, watched by dozens of eyes that kept a careful distance. I twisted in his grip to look through the door.

The sky was black beyond the second seal, and I could not see the stars. I turned away from the porthole, away from the nothingness of space where my mother had died. I faced Adam. "You have nothing left," I began, but he scoffed.

"I have an entire Ark slaved to my blood. What do you

have? An army? Armies can be killed. Do you know how many people are about to die, Char?"

"You can't get out of this, Adam," I said softly. "They're going to save this Ark from you while they still can. They'd be fools not to. You *will* die. Neither one of us can stop it. But you can save the North American Ark. You're the only one who can."

He stumbled back, feeling for a keypad. Searching for a weapon. What was the play here?

Wait, no. He was steadying himself. He didn't know what to do next.

He was afraid.

And then it hit me. I had one final play. One last move. I slammed my fist into the first seal on the hangar. It sucked open, taking what was left of my heart and soul into its void. I clenched my fist, but my hand did not shake. I did not waver.

It wouldn't do to lose my courage now, at the end of everything.

"I can't stop them, Adam," I said again. "This is where you die. But I will make the journey with you. Decouple your heartbeat from life support, and I'll come with you."

Adam's eyes were wild. He glanced through the porthole and back to me. "Now, that's interesting."

I stepped closer to him, and, taking his hand in mine, led him across the seal. The keypad was out of reach once we crossed the threshold. I did not take my eyes from Adam's even as I spoke to Isaiah. "Close the airlock." There was steel in my voice. It pleased me.

I could hear the tightness of Isaiah's throat, his mouth. I pictured his fingers wrapped hard around his gun. I thought about my mother. I finally saw her strength in me. "*Do it. Do it, Ise.*"

When at last there was no response, I turned to him.

Isaiah's eyes gleamed silver, but his hand was unsteady, and the barrel of the gun began to waver. "I—I can't," he said. "I'm sorry, little bird. I can't do it."

"You have to." I tasted the words and found that my voice was strong. "*To go back is nothing but death. I will yet go forward.*"

At this, his face crumpled. The gun fell to his side. "You read my book."

I gave him a sad smile. "Seemed the thing to do at the time. Know your enemy, and all that."

"I can't. I can't."

His sadness nearly broke me. I wanted to be like stone, like a statue. I wanted to be like the frozen wind that shaped the earth to its will.

But I was none of those things. I was flesh and bone, and weak enough at that. I was small.

Nevertheless, it was enough. I only had to be strong for a little longer. I looked back at Adam. "You can close it, can't you? You can control the seal."

"You don't really want to die, do you, Char?" Adam asked. His voice was small, too. Like a child.

"No," I breathed. "I'm afraid. But I am sick of fighting."

At that, he opened his shirt. Long, thin wires protruded from every side of a small metal box on his chest, like a millipede. A few of the wires went into his skin, anchoring the box into place. Its top slid off. "Okay," he said shakily, pressing a series of buttons I couldn't follow. A moment passed, and he looked at me, pale-faced and quiet. "Okay. I accept." He aimed the device at the door, and it hissed shut, sealing us to our fate.

Isaiah rushed to the panel, and the lock clicked just as

he reached it. "NO!" He slammed a fist on the window, and I jumped in spite of myself. "No!"

I met his gaze, feeling very much like an uprooted tree. "Confirm it's done," I said to him. "Go, Ise. Confirm that our Ark is safe."

He was breathing hard, but at last he nodded and disappeared, and I was alone with Adam. I had to keep him here. Not forever. But for a little while.

"You know, we always talk about my family. We never talk about yours," I said.

Adam didn't answer.

"What was your father like?" I said.

"You would have liked him," he said, his mind elsewhere. "He always told me not to fight."

I looked around the room. I had to keep him distracted before he changed his mind. "And your mom?"

Adam returned to the moment long enough to give me a bitter frown. "She told me not to lose."

"I'm sorry about your sister," I said suddenly. "I tried to save her. I did."

He thought about that for a moment. "I never hurt you," he said finally. "On the Ark. I didn't let anyone touch you." His hands went to his sleeve, the box, his forehead, fidgeting. He'd only ever been a child, but now, his fear made him like a little boy. "I didn't want to be alone."

"It's okay," I said softly. "It's almost over."

He breathed harder and took a step closer. I jerked back instinctively. His face went hard. "A deal is a deal," he said. "Unless you have another trick up your sleeve."

"I'm clean out of tricks, Adam."

He stood close, but he didn't touch me, and I realized I'd begun to shake. So much for bravery.

Isaiah appeared at the window, surrounded by gendarmes. "So?" I shouted. "Is it done?"

He didn't answer. I heard a sound like a cross between a slap and a keyboard tap and realized that he was trying to open the seal. I glanced at Adam, who shook his head. "They can't get in here."

"Okay," I said, wishing I were stronger. "Okay."

A soldier grabbed Isaiah, pulling him backwards, and another man appeared at the window. "I can confirm that the slave program is no longer running. The North American Ark is free." He paused. "Go with God, Lieutenant."

Adam looked at me, taking in my shaking jaw, and put his arms around me. He was taller than I, but his head rested on my shoulder. I went limp, then stiffened. I was so close. I couldn't let him get out of this, no matter what came next. So I returned the embrace.

"I had a dream you were drowning," he said distantly, his voice muffled against my shoulder. "You and Amiel. Over and over. And I could only save one of you."

"It was never your job to save me, Adam."

He shook his head without lifting it. "I thought I could make you understand. No fighting for *five years*, Char. No one else could fix the atmosphere, either. It had to be me. It had to." He straightened suddenly, then pressed a few keys on his wire box, leaned across me, and slammed his fist into the last seal of the airlock.

There was a quick pop followed by an even shorter *hiss*. I heard myself begin to scream, but the void entered the room, entered *me*. I curled up into a ball, shutting my mouth and eyes as hard as I could, and pressed my fingers into my ears.

I felt Adam shove my shoulders back, giving himself about

a foot of distance, then kick me, *hard*, in my chest. I went sailing backwards as the outer seal sucked closed. The darkness claimed me. The void was my inheritance. In a moment, I would be like my mother.

The thought of her face made me gasp.

I took a breath, panting, and realized that I *could* breathe. The inner door was open.

Hands took me, pulling me into the ship like a baby. I heard the inner door suck closed, but I couldn't relax. I couldn't open my eyes, my ears, my mouth. I stayed curled up until I felt Isaiah's hands. He was shaking me, saying my name again and again. He said something about West, too, but I couldn't make it out.

I opened my eyes slowly. The world was harsh and bright. Soldiers crouched around me as others were glued to the inner porthole, unable to believe that Adam was gone. They were saying things I didn't understand, and I squinted at them. The man who'd spoken to me through the window turned to his troops and nodded. A cheer broke out throughout the corridor.

When Isaiah saw my eyes, he smiled. I tried to sit and found that I couldn't. All around us, the soldiers were overcome with relief and laughter. But we did not cheer. I was tired. So tired. My eyes pulled closed, and I did not try to stop them.

It was over.

# Twenty-four

I woke up angry.

Another gurney. Another handcuff, no doubt.

I jerked my good arm and saw that it was free. Hearing me stir, my brother West looked up from his seat in a wheelchair facing me.

Another dream, then.

"She's awake!" he said. "Char!"

I frowned at him, furious. How dare he haunt my dreams so soon. How dare he seem so happy when we were still apart.

My father came into view next to my brother, relief etched into every line on his face. I twisted my head painfully and saw that we were joined by Eren, Isaiah, Cecelia, Maxx, and even Charles. They stood in a semicircle around my bed, watching me. Except for Eren, that is. He was horizontal and covered in white, but his blue eyes found mine immediately.

A strange dream.

"A moment, please," said a familiar voice over my shoulder. I looked up to see crystal blue eyes and a tight blonde bun.

"Doctor," I whispered. "I'm hallucinating."

She laughed, and I wondered if perhaps this wasn't a dream. West was older than he ever was in my dreams, and his voice was deeper. "West?" I said. "How?"

He leaned in carefully in spite of the doctor's disapproving glance and squeezed my bad arm.

"Isaiah saw the broom before Adam moved it," he said. "When I insisted on going back in, he gave me his uniform."

"His uniform?"

"The bullets don't pierce the fabric, Char. Remember?"

I thought about that for a long time.

And then I began to cry.

My leg was set in a cast the next day. I'd broken my fibula in the storm. For the time being, I could not stand.

Eren did not leave my side.

For one thing, he wasn't able to. He'd broken several bones in his upper body and was contained in the worst-looking traction device I'd ever seen.

For another, I wasn't about to let him. We'd spent enough time on other people's schedules. It would be awhile before I let him out of my sight again.

Charles visited me alone the next day. It was an attempt at a friendship, an olive branch, but I found myself bitter. He'd locked my father up while Adam ran free. I saw in his face that he still didn't know what to make of me. So I asked him why he was there, and he said he'd promised An he'd visit.

"An." The name brought with it a sense of unease, of unpredictability. "She never fired her missiles after all."

"A curious move, given what we thought," Charles mused. "But I have my guesses as to why."

"Care to let me in on those?" I asked.

"Actually, I think it came down to you," Charles said quietly. "She never wanted to fire in the first place, obviously. But Adam sent her blueprints for an electromagnetic field generator, and she knew she couldn't build it without repurposing her warheads."

"That was a test," I said. "He wanted us to kill each other."

"Perhaps," Charles allowed. "But her scientists have reviewed the plans. It seems a plausible mechanism. And so she waited, hoping we'd prevail. Thanks to you, we did."

"You weren't so bad yourself," I said, offering him a smile.

"Thank you, my dear." There was an awkward pause. "We've extended amnesty to you and your family, by the way."

At this, I gave a dark laugh. "So I'm finally legit? I can't believe that's all it took."

"You'll have the option to return to the North American Ark, of course, but should you decide to stay..."

"Thank you, Charles." I offered him my hand, and he shook it. "I appreciate that."

"There is one other thing," he said, hesitating. "We've had a special meeting of the Council."

I nodded, waiting.

"We're not staying, Char. This Ark won't colonize Eirenea. We're going back to Earth."

"Back to Earth? Charles. There *is* no Earth."

He took a deep breath. "Not as it was, no. Its polarity was destroyed, and the continents have undergone significant changes. As it stands now, no life is possible. But we've been in contact with Ark Five all along, you know."

"Noooo," I sucked my teeth. "You don't say."

"Yes, well." He cleared his throat. "They are of the opinion that in time, we can colonize it. The South American Ark is going back, too."

"Colonize Earth," I said softly. "Home."

He looked at me. "You know, I'm really not sure what that means anymore."

I took his hand again, giving him a little squeeze. I wished him well. "Me neither. Not for awhile now. Me neither."

By the end of the day, I'd moved my bed against Eren's. It had been a difficult operation, since Eren hadn't been able to help, but seeing me struggle, the doctor lent a hand. She even removed one of the guardrails between us, cautioning me not to touch him. We stayed up nights, talking. Even when he was like this, crippled, immobile, broken into pieces, he made me feel safe.

He had plans. Hopes. Things I'd never heard him talk about before. He wanted a family one day. He wanted a garden. He wanted to stand on Eirenea and build up a mighty city. Not as the leader, or the president, but as a builder.

He wanted a thousand things, and he wanted them with me.

And gradually, by the third or fourth night, it hit me that he intended to keep on living. It occurred to me that I wasn't sure what I wanted yet, except to be with him. So I supposed I would keep on living, too. Maybe one day, I'd find dreams of my own again.

The thought wasn't so bad.

# Twenty-five

*One year later*

I stood to face my family. They filed in quickly, wrapping me in embrace after embrace, with Ce-ya taking more than her fair share, making my heart beat all the way up into my throat. Long gone were the baby rolls and gummy grin. In their place stood a confident girl who loved to laugh and play tricks on her unsuspecting aunt. Who loved her family with every atom of her fierce, tiny being, including me.

Especially me. I stared a moment longer, thinking of the woman she would become. At this rate, and knowing her parents, she'd be a force to reckon with by the time she hit sixteen. Watching her grow over the past year had been among the deepest joys of my life. The thought made me smile in spite of the wrenching pressure around my heart.

Maxx, too, gave me an unending series of hugs, and I soaked them in. He was tall—as tall as his father—and I smiled as I tilted my face to his. I hadn't known it was possible to love anyone as much as I loved West, but these two proved me wrong a hundred times a day.

My family was leaving me.

230

The High Council of the EuroArk could not resist the pull of Earth. Ark Five had long since returned to the destroyed planet, mining what was left of its resources and colonizing its airspace, one bright new ship after another. In time, they would terraform the surface.

Our race was going home. Part of it, anyway. Anyone who wished would receive citizenship and safe passage aboard one of the two Arks leaving Eirenea. The current generation would die in space, warm in their beds, at the end of long lives. But their children might walk among the trees again. A final glance at Maxx took my breath away. He and West farmed the reconstructed biosphere together. One day he might farm the Earth beside his own sons and daughters.

Of course West had chosen to remain with the biosphere. It had been his life's dream, and now, it was his life's work to rebuild it. I understood.

In the end, my father had chosen my brother and the promise of the old world. I did not blame him. The EuroArk's vision was bright, alluring. As a species, we would colonize our first home, rebuilding its poles and replanting its trees, and who knew where we'd go from there? Our race was spreading out over the solar system. We would not be defeated by a meteor—or a madman—ever again.

So the biosphere went with the EuroArk, now that its seeds were planted on Eirenea as well. West and his family went with the biosphere, and that was that. The constant anger I'd lived with since childhood had drained from my heart long ago, and in its place, I felt only love. Love for Mars, with whom I'd buried a portion of my very soul. Love for my niece and my nephew. Love for West and my father, the only people alive who remembered my mother's smile.

Love hurt.

Eren stood behind me, and I was happy, if not blissful. *Happy*, I thought. That was the right word. His place was with me, and mine with him. We had a lifetime to figure out the rest. He'd been right, years ago, when he'd placed his mother's ring on my hand for the second and final time: We made each other strong. The thought would surely be enough to bolster me through the coming days, if only barely.

"You look good, Charlotte." My father hugged me again, and this time, I let myself relax, feeling his arms around me for the last time. He squeezed a little harder than before, and lingered longer than even Ce-ya.

"You too, Dad." I drew a breath in sharply, then bit my lip as hard as I could. I did not want to cry. Since this was the last time they'd ever see me, I didn't want to be remembered like some kind of mess. In spite of everything, I wanted so badly to be strong for them. To be someone they could respect.

Most of all, when they told stories of me over dinner, laughing and acting out the best parts together, I wanted them to be happy, too.

"Charlotte, we're—" he began, then broke off. "I just wanted—*we* wanted—to let you know that—"

His eyes and nose were raw, and it hit me that he had cried for me. We met each other's eyes, and I knew that he'd miss me as much as I him. "You don't have to go, Dad. It's not too late."

"It's not too late for you, either. You can still join *us*."

I wanted to laugh, but it wasn't funny. We really were so stubborn, the two of us.

I shook my head. "My life is here. There's still so much to do. The last draft of the Treaty is slated for next week, and that's just the beginning. I'm really—I'm making a difference, Dad. Isaiah wants me making planetfall tonight, just to make sure everything's ready." To be needed. To be necessary, even for a moment. It was more than I'd hoped for.

"He has so much support, he'll be president forever," said my dad.

"Ten years, and he's out. There's gonna be a whole thing in the new constitution about it, or he won't sign it. But there's plenty of work to go around till then. He's building something great, Dad. We all are."

All at once, my father stood up straight before me. He placed his hands on my shoulders. "Charlotte. Promise me that you will never forget that your father loves you. That I am proud of you. I'm so—" He broke off again, but West stepped forward to stand beside him, and he became strong again. "I'm so proud that you are my daughter."

Eren was next to me, his arm around my waist, and my courage did not fail. "I promise, Dad," I said.

There was a knock at the door, and my chief of staff poked his head in. "Excuse me, Senator," he said. "The hopper's ready when you are."

"Thanks, Kellan." It was too late to hide my face, so I gave him a weak smile. He had his mother's eyes.

My dad turned to leave, stopping only to shake Eren's hand, then pulled him into an embrace. They spoke into each other's ears, and then my family was gone.

All except West.

"Char," he said.

I made a sound like a laugh and a heavy sniff, and felt my tears hit my collarbone. "West. I love you. You know that."

His face was red. I could barely see the child he'd been in the set of his brow, his jaw. He seemed to me a stronger man than I'd yet realized. "Always. You know I love you too, sis."

I took a breath. "I hope you make it all the way back. I hope that your children see ten thousand sunsets, and that they will stand on the Earth and know that it is their home. And that it is precious, no matter where else we go." I was crying now. There was no stopping it. "I—I want all the best things in the world for them. For you."

He laughed, and I saw that he was weeping. My strength faltered at last, so he held my arms, keeping me upright. "Most of all," I said finally, "I hope you will remember me. The good things."

He hugged me—my last embrace with my West—and kissed me on the cheek. "They were all good things, Tarry."

And then he was gone.

# Twenty-six

At the hour of the launch, I fastened the straps of the hopper's jump seat myself. My luggage and my team rode aboard the last OPT—On-Planet Transport—to leave the Ark, but Isaiah and I had some final plots and plans to hammer out regarding the transition, so I was going with him on a hopper.

We were so close to walking on Eirenea that I could taste it. An hour from now, we'd land in the Asian Sea, which An had poured out onto the surface of the planet half a year ago. It was smaller than it had seemed on board her Ark, but the salt and water synths were steadily pumping, fed by the mining operations we'd begun six months earlier. The sea grew bigger by the day.

Like, *fractionally* bigger, but still.

I couldn't suppress the excitement that bubbled up inside me. I'd seen delicate rows of crops peeking through the clouds as we sailed overhead in orbit just last week.

Eirenea was colonized. All that remained were the pilgrims.

"Ark Two to Everest. Come in, Char."

I flicked the comm switch and smiled. "Well, hello there. I thought you were in meetings all afternoon."

Eren's voice filled the tiny cabin. "They can wait. No one expects me to focus while my wife's making planetfall."

I fiddled with the ring on my good hand and aimed a twisted smile at the speaker. "We said goodbye ten minutes ago. I don't even miss you yet!"

"You do. And you will."

"Yeah, you're probably right. Any word from my family?" I immediately regretted asking. Now Eren would worry about me. Of course they hadn't sent a transmission yet. We'd only said goodbye an hour ago. Those would come soon enough, and often.

There was a pause, and Eren cleared his throat. "Oh, only about four megs," he joked. "At least three of that is from Ce-ya. Should hit your screen when you're in range of the city."

"I'll be fine, Eren," I said, responding to the note of concern in his voice that had nothing to do with the Treaty of Eirenea. "My family is happy. I am happy."

There was a pause, and I heard his smile through the speaker. "Copy that. Everest out."

"Everest out." I leaned back, waiting for Isaiah. He kept a busy schedule, and I didn't mind the time. I wanted to think. I turned my attention to the panel and let out a breath, piece by piece, until I was empty.

The North American settlement was over a thousand miles from the Asian one, but transports ran between the two daily. They were massive and growing every day.

As Trade Commissioner, Eren ran a small team tasked with coordinating and protecting the ongoing negotiations between them. Like the other task forces formed after the second Treaty was signed, this one was composed mostly of former soldiers and relied heavily on military-grade equipment that had been repurposed. He was happy, too. He'd spent decades preparing for war and devastation. Now, he prepared for a lifetime of peace and plenty. It suited him.

My role as Senator was less straightforward, and I found that it suited me as well. I had never been able to see the world as Eren did, all bright and clear and full of straight edges, though I loved him for it. I'd made my home in the gray for far too long, and it was here that I worked toward the splendid future Eren saw around every corner.

The hopper jostled as Isaiah slid through the hatch. He landed in his seat in a single fluid motion, like a cat. "Hey," he said.

"Hey."

"You ready?" he asked.

"Yeah." I nodded, and his eyes searched mine, unsatisfied.

"No screaming," he said solemnly.

I laughed, recalling our first trip in a hopper together. "No screaming."

He locked the hatch, saving the head restraints for last, then gave my bad arm a squeeze. I tried to return the squeeze out of instinct, but of course I had no hand on that arm, and I couldn't. I wondered if I'd ever get used to missing a part of myself.

Somehow, I doubted it.

"Did you know that Bunyan wrote a sequel?" he said suddenly.

I took a second, waiting for the words to register. They didn't. "Who?"

"*The Pilgrim's Progress*. There's a sequel."

I shook my head, utterly confused, and loosened the restraint again. I couldn't get comfortable. "If you had any idea how long it took me to get through the first one," I muttered, "you wouldn't be telling me this. Unless you're planning to lock me in a cell with nothing else to read, like last time."

"I like to think we're past that," he said. The humor played out under the deepest tones of his voice.

I rolled my eyes and gave a half-snort. "Okay, fine, Mr. *President*. What happens in the sequel? The pilgrim's story pretty much ends in the first one."

"It does." He gave a satisfied glance at the dash. "Part two is about his family."

I wrenched the restraint off my head. I hated that thing. Nothing fit. "His family."

"They have to make a journey, too."

I had nothing to say to that, so he popped a switch on the dash, and the hangar was filled with the light hum of the engine. "Well," he said, his voice supremely mellow, in contrast to the sharpness in mine. "Time to go."

Isaiah took us out into the stars with impressive efficiency. I couldn't grip his hand, obviously, but he didn't take his off my arm. I'd resigned myself to being a nervous flyer a long time ago. We were just about to begin the fall when Isaiah turned to me with a devilish look in his eye. "Are you ready for the meteors?" he said.

What was left of my nerve seemed to flitter off into space. "Meteors? Plural?"

He smiled, as though we were sharing a joke. "A shower, in fact. The space debris trailing Ark Three is scheduled to make planetfall about the same time that we do."

Ark Three had reached Eirenea's airspace a few days earlier. It was a personnel drop for anyone who wanted to remain on Eirenea before they returned to Earth forever. Our hopper swung around, bringing Eirenea into view.

"Meteors," I said. "Who'd have thought. Life is strange."

"It is," he agreed solemnly. "And that's not the strangest part. They're sending out signals."

"The meteors? What kind of signals?"

He shrugged. "No elevated radioactivity. Even if it's weapons, it won't survive the atmosphere. It's something from Earth, but whatever it is, it'll be destroyed by the time we get out of the water."

I squinted out the window, reminding myself to stay calm. Trying not to think of how small the hopper was, how thin its shields. Slender ribbons of red and orange lit Eirenea's delicate atmosphere. There had to be a hundred at least, and the meteor shower was just getting started.

When we were moments from the atmosphere, about to become a meteor ourselves, the comm crackled to life. "Planetfall in five, Mr. President."

"Copy that, Chiro. I'm all set. Any read on that signal?"

"Yes, sir," came the reply. "It's an auto-transmission of some sort. Intentional. It's... it's a list, Mr. President. We haven't worked through the meaning yet."

"A list," Isaiah said, his expression darkening. "Read it to me."

"Yes, sir. Every signal is different, but they're all lists. They repeat on a loop. Starting with the first signal we caught: scream, persistence, Guernica—"

Isaiah frowned. "This is concerning, Major. Do we have another?"

"Yes, sir. Starting the second signal we found: Odalisque, Napoleon, Venus, gothic, Olympia—"

"How long are these lists?" Isaiah asked.

"Long, sir. Maybe a hundred in a set. Sir, planetfall is imminent."

I shut my eyes against the ominous streaks of fire and braced myself for the fall. My grip on the armrest became shaky, but something tingled in the back of my mind, bringing with it a conversation I'd had years ago. I knew once gravity caught us, the shell of the hopper would burn, and after that, we'd be in freefall until the chute deployed. My near-terror clouded out the memory I sought to retrieve.

Isaiah continued as though we weren't about to fling ourselves into a body of water several miles below. "I'm concerned it could be some kind of biological weapon. Some strains we haven't heard of, that we couldn't test for."

The shields around the hopper began to glow. We were entering the atmosphere. "Ark Three denies knowledge, sir."

"Is that right?" Isaiah said skeptically. The glow grew to flames. My pulse pounded through my arms and legs, turning them to jelly.

"Sir, your chute will deploy in three, two, *one.*"

The hopper slammed forward, and my head caught against the strap.

"Prepare for impact in thirty seconds, Mr. President."

"Copy that, Chiro. Does the team have any—quiet, Char, calm down. Does the team have—excuse me," he said, shouting now. "Char. Please."

I stopped screaming long enough to take a breath. The ocean spread before me, and even with the drag of the landing chute, it was coming in fast. My mind cleared only long enough for me to convey a single thought. "ART!" I said, still screaming.

"Senator?" came the voice. "Impact in five—"

"I AM NEVER FLYING AGAIN. IT'S ART. IT'S *ART,*" I screeched, then took one last breath before we hit and continued to scream for all I was worth. "IT'S ART OH NO OH-AAAHHH."

Isaiah let out a great whoop, and his face was full of joy. "Here... we... GO!"

The hopper struck the sea, jolting me hard enough to cause a momentary break in my screams, and we spun out across the surface of the water before crashing beneath the waves.

The water hissed as it struck the burning capsule and sucked closed over our heads, and the hopper transitioned perfectly into phib mode. Isaiah gave me a look of mock-reproval and began making preparations for the surface. I took a minute to gather what remained of my senses and recalled, too late, my promise not to scream.

"Sorry," I said meekly.

But he just shook his head, laughing. We were home.

# Epilogue

*I am standing on the shore of a new life. Eirenea stretches out before me. The sea beats against my legs, faster than the oceans of Earth. Isaiah surfaces behind me, his silver eyes full of wonder. For the moment, we do not speak.*

*This planet is warm, like a greenhouse. Too warm for sleeves. I shuck my jacket and dip down into the water once again. I can't float. It's probably because of my shoes. When I emerge, Isaiah has made it to the edge of the shore. The waters lick at his boots.*

*Overhead, the pink-orange sky begins to burn with delicate streaks of red and white-yellow. As promised, the meteors do not survive the enhanced atmo shields. We are awash in the light of their fire.*

*"So. Art," he says. He does not look back to me.*

*"Pods and pods of art. Thousands of works. Charles chose them, designed the pods. He thought they'd stay near Earth, maybe be discovered one day. It's everything he wanted to save before he built the nursery instead."*

*"Originals." It's not a question. I do not answer. For the moment, Isaiah is lost in thought. "Stand with me here, Char," he says. "We'll take the first step together."*

242

*I slosh through the churning tide to take my place at his side. Our settlement looms large on the horizon, and only half-lit as yet. Ours are not the first human steps in this alien world. We're not the first explorers here, the first builders. We will not be the last.*

*The rocks sink beneath my feet, and he reaches out to steady me. "Earth below. Fire above. The city ahead." He offers me a smile, and I do my best to return it. He shoulders his pack and takes the lead, stuffing his space skin through a strap, pulling the mouthpiece out of the helmet, around his shoulder, and up to his lips, breathing in the oxygen.*

*Soon, the forests and the ocean will supply more oxygen than we could ever need. We will build cabins among the trees and watch the pines grow tall around us. We walk together without speaking as the art burns to ashes overhead.*

*It will take years to restore the things we have lost.*

*Around me, the fire-streaked sky is lit by the first tendrils of dawn. My first sunrise in eight years. I will shake the persistent dusk from my mind. I will yet go forward.*

*We reach the city, and I remember the first time I met Ce-ya and the feel of her fat, tiny arms against my neck, and my heart sinks down into the earth beneath me. But the inner lock opens, and I am beckoned forth. I am needed. I have Eren. In time, we will build a family of our own, and we will choose them, every day of their lives. And they will know it. I swallow at the thought, pressing my ribs out, straining against the tightness in my chest, in my throat, but its grip is too deep.*

*I will yet go forward. I can still be strong without them.*

*Their faces run through my mind, over and over, like the waves of the ocean, and I smile in spite of myself.*

Laura Liddell Nolen

I can still be strong because of them.

"*Welcome home, Senator.*" *A bright young woman wearing a simple green robe extends a hand, and I move forward to grasp it. I cannot help the grin that spreads across my face. I lift my chin and step into the city, where Ise is waiting.*

*We have work to do.*

# Acknowledgements

Thanks to God for loving me. I'm also grateful for the following people for enabling (and even encouraging!) my writing habit over the past several years: Will Nolen, Morris Liddell, Ben Morris, and Jenna Wolf. They've lit the path I've travelled alongside Char from beginning to end.

Enormous thanks to those who have read my work and taken the time to write to me about it, or who have even gone so far as to leave a review. I'm deeply touched.

Thank you, Natasha Bardon. Thanks to all the lovely people at HarperVoyager UK, past and present, including Eleanor Ashfield, Jack Butler, Rachel Winterbottom, Lily Cooper, and Jack Renninson, who have helped in the promotion and publication of this series.

Thank you to this book's aunts and uncles, who have made a point of supporting me, and thanks to my family! (Hi, Mom.) The list is long, but here are a few names off the top: Will, Ava, Liam, and Oscar. Lesha Grant and Aundrea Leven. Courtney, Alex, Jennifer, and Jordana. I love you!